Tobias
The Carmichaels
Leigh Fenty

Chapter One

"Goodnight, Random Guy."

T obias studied the clear liquid in the bottom of his glass and tried to remember when he'd started drinking rum exclusively. It was before the damn horse rolled over him and shattered his left leg. But that incident seemed to be the catalyst for increasing the volume and frequency of his rum consumption.

He drained the glass and stared at the television set mounted behind the bar. There was a football game on. The sound was off, but he was fine with that. He was never much for football.

The bartender glanced at him. "Do you want me to turn it up?"

"No. Not a fan. But if you can find a good rodeo, I might be interested."

The bartender laughed. "Probably not going to happen at ten p.m."

"I guess you're right."

When a woman entered the room and approached the bar, she drew both of the men's attention when she took a seat two stools down from Tobias. He nodded at her as the bartender moved toward her. She wasn't the type of woman you would expect to find sitting at a bar alone. She was very attractive, and nicely dressed in slacks and a fitted leather jacket. The dark burgundy color of her jacket complimented her auburn hair, which was pulled into a high ponytail hanging half-way down her back.

The bartender gave her a smile. "What can I get you?"

"Rum and Coke, please."

He looked at Tobias. "Do you need a refill, too?"

Tobias nodded. "And put the lady's drink on my tab."

She looked at him with light blue eyes that seemed unnatural in color, but somehow completed the whole package. "Thank you. But I can pay for my own drinks. I don't need some random guy buying them for me."

Tobias smiled. "Okay. Would you like to pay for mine?"

"No. Let's both pay for our own drinks."

He nodded. "Sounds good."

The bartender poured the drinks and delivered them. When he saw the woman watching the game, he offered to turn it up for her.

She shook her head. "No, thank you. I'm not a fan."

Tobias grinned and looked at her. "Seems we have a lot in common."

She took a drink, then turned toward him. "How do you figure?"

"Well. We're both here alone in a bar. We both drink rum. And neither of us gives a damn about football."

The corners of her mouth curved up slightly, but stopped just short of a smile. "Seems that would describe quite a few people."

He shrugged. "Still. Pretty coincidental."

"Okay. I'll bite. What do you think it means?"

"I don't know. But you could scooch over a couple stools, and we could try to figure it out."

"Sounds like a ploy to me."

He took a drink. "Suit yourself. I don't care much one way or the other."

She studied him for a moment, then picked up her drink and moved to the stool next to him.

"So you think your disinterest is going to get me interested?"

He grinned, again. "You're sitting next to me, aren't you?"

She gave him a genuine smile, then laughed as she raised her glass. "Yes, I am."

Tobias tapped her glass with his. "Cheers."

She looked at his jeans, western cut shirt, and boots. "So, are you a real cowboy? Or are you a weekend cowboy who likes to dress the part?"

"Fourth generation cowboy." He offered his hand. "The name is Guy. Random Guy."

She shook her head. "Now *that's* coincidental." She took his hand. "Random Girl."

He held her hand a moment before letting go. "So, Miss Girl, what brings you to this empty bar in Malady Springs?"

"Is that where I'm at? I figured it was so far in the middle of nowhere it didn't even have a name."

"Compared to where I'm from, this is a thriving metropolis."

"So, are there actually springs here?"

"Used to be." He took a sip of rum. "Dried up a few years back."

"That's sad."

"You didn't answer my question."

She took a drink. "No personal questions, if you don't mind."

"I told you I was a cowboy. It's only fair for you to answer at least one personal question."

She tapped her modestly manicured nails on the bar. "I suppose I could tell you what I do."

He turned toward her. "No wait. Let me guess." He studied her for a moment. "You're not a hooker, are you?"

"Excuse me?"

"Just kidding. An accountant."

She laughed. "I believe I'm insulted. I'd almost rather you thought I was a hooker."

"I only guessed that because you look smart. Let me try again." He hesitated while he pondered the possibilities. "Executive secretary."

"You think I look like a secretary?"

"I can't win." He took another drink. "So, maybe you're the boss. The CEO. Whatever that is."

"You guessed it. I'm the CEO of a very successful accounting firm in...San Antonio."

He shook his head. "Seems we're from two different worlds."

"It would seem so."

He faced the bar again. "Would you like another round?"

"Yes. I would."

Tobias waved at the bartender. "Two more, please." He glanced at his new friend. "Separate tabs."

They spent the next two hours talking, but never shared anything personal. It was a game and both of them played it well. When the bartender told them it was last call, they both declined a final drink.

Tobias turned in his seat. "So, Random. Can I call you by your first name? Seems we've reached that point."

She smiled. "This has been a very enjoyable evening. It was unexpected."

He took her hand. "It doesn't have to end. We could go get coffee at a twenty-four-hour coffee shop."

She squeezed his hand, then let go. "I'm afraid it does. If I drink coffee now, I'll be up all night."

"You don't have to drink coffee. We could eat. A burger? Bacon and eggs?"

She got to her feet. "You're very sweet. And it's very tempting. But I need to call it a night."

He stood, too, and laid a hundred-dollar bill on the bar.

She looked at it. "I thought I was paying for my own drinks."

"You can throw a few bucks on top of that. It probably doesn't quite cover it."

She opened her purse and took out a twenty. "Let's make sure the bartender gets a nice tip."

Tobias nodded. "At least let me walk you to your car."

She took his arm, and they headed for the entrance. When they got outside, he stopped on the sidewalk. "So, where did you park?"

She nodded across the street. "In the motel parking lot. Right in front of my room." The street was empty, and they walked across to the Malady Springs Motel. "Room thirteen. On the end."

Tobias walked with her to the end room. "Thank you for a lovely evening."

"You're not going to drive, are you?"

He shook his head and took a motel key out of his pocket. He held it up. "Room eleven."

She smiled. "Good night, Random Guy."

He nodded. "Miss Girl."

She opened her door, and he walked down two doors to his room. He glanced back as she disappeared inside, then went into his room and sat on the end of the bed. "Holy shit." He laid back. For the first time since he met Cassidy, he felt like he'd just experienced something phenomenal and life-changing. He sighed. "Too bad you'll never see her again."

At the sound of a light knock on the door, he sat up. "Impossible." He went to the door and opened it, then cocked his head and smiled.

"Hey, Guy." He opened the door wider, and she came into the room. "Turns out I'm not ready to call it a night, after all." She put her arms around his neck and pulled him in for a kiss.

He looked at her. "You like being the boss, don't you?"

They backed into his room and he kicked the door closed. She started unbuttoning his shirt.

He kissed her, then smiled. "I really wasn't angling for this. I just wanted to go to Denny's."

"Random Guy."

"Yeah?"

"Stop talking."

"Yes, ma'am."

Tobias woke up when the woman he'd just spent an exhilarating and intense night with got out of the bed. He still didn't know her name. But it didn't really matter. He reached for her hand.

"What are you doing?"

"I need to go."

He raised up onto an elbow. "Is this the part where you regret what happened and slink off?"

"No regrets. No slinking." She bent down and kissed him. "I'll never forget the night I spent with my random guy."

He grinned. "I was pretty good. Wasn't I?"

"Don't ruin it."

She tried to retrieve her hand, but he held tight. "Before you go. Tell me something that's true. Just one thing for me to hold on to."

She looked at him for a moment. "I'll tell you two things. One true and one not true. You can decide which one you want to believe."

He let go of her hand, then leaned back against the headboard and stuffed a pillow behind his back. "Interesting. I like that. I'll do the same."

"You go first."

He thought for a moment. "I've never ridden a horse in my life. And I went to Yale."

"Hmm. Interesting. Okay. I didn't go to college. And I have a son."

"Wow."

She picked up her clothes. "I've got to go."

"Board meeting?"

"Something a lot more fun than that."

"It's been...surreal, Boss Lady."

Chapter Two

"Are you a real cowboy?"

Cassidy waved at her friend, Gemma, as she and her boyfriend pulled in front of the house. They'd be staying in the guest rooms for the week of festivities leading up to the wedding. Her wedding. The last seven months had been a whirlwind. Deacon had asked her to marry him a week before Thanksgiving. But it wasn't official until he gave her a ring for Christmas. It was beautiful and way too expensive. But she loved it. And she loved that he wanted to give it to her.

Cassidy smiled as Gemma got out of the car. "You're here. How was the trip?"

"It was fine." She glanced at her boyfriend, Preston as he joined them. "We took our time." Gemma looked around. "This place is fantastic."

"Isn't it beautiful?" Cassidy looked toward the car. "Where's Riley?"

"He's asleep in the backseat."

Gemma took her hand. "And where's your handsome cowboy?"

"He and his brother had to ride out to the herd. There was a problem with a cow and her calf."

"You're really a rancher's wife, aren't you?"

"Not quite. In a few days, yes!"

Gemma took hold of Preston's arm. "You remember Preston, right?"

Cassidy shook with him. "Of course. I'm glad you could come with Gemma."

"Wouldn't miss it." He seemed a bit uncomfortable and out of place, and Cassidy wondered if he'd ever been off a paved road, much less on a ranch. She'd known Gemma since college, and she could never quite understand her relationship with Preston. He was quiet and studious, while she was outgoing and loved to be adventurous. They were a mismatched pair.

When Cassidy spotted a rider coming across the field, she took a moment to determine which Carmichael brother it was. She'd learned to recognize their riding styles from a distance. Tobias was always a little stiff, in order to favor his leg.

"Well, here's Tobias. I wonder where Deacon is."

Tobias rode to the barn then dismounted and tied his horse to a rail before crossing the yard to Cassidy and her friends. He knew she was expecting her best friend from college, who would be her maid of honor. On the way, he removed his gloves and tucked them into his pocket. As he got closer, he stopped walking. There was no way he was seeing what he was seeing.

Cassidy went to him and took his arm. "Come meet Gemma and Preston."

He numbly allowed her to lead him the rest of the way and he offered his hand to the woman he hadn't been able to stop thinking about.

"Hi." He met her blue eyes, that conveyed surprise and then panic. "Tobias Carmichael."

She gave him a small smile, then hesitated before saying, "Gemma Stone." She glanced at the man standing next to her, then looked at Tobias again. He couldn't quite read what her eyes were saying now. "This is Preston Lancaster." She took a breath and looked away from Tobias. "My boyfriend."

Tobias tried not to react as he felt himself turning toward the man and shaking hands with him. Somehow he managed to add, "Welcome to the Starlight Ranch."

When the door to the backseat opened up, they all turned to watch a boy of about six or seven climb out and look around. Well, now he knew which of the things she'd told him in the hotel room were true. He looked just like her. He had the same blue eyes. But his hair was dark and wavy.

He ran over to Gemma. "We're here?"

She smiled at him. "Yes, honey. We made it."

"Can I see a horse?"

"Soon. Let's go inside and get settled in first."

"Okay." He looked at Tobias. "Are you a real cowboy?"

Tobias removed his hat and glanced at Gemma. "Yes, I am."

Gemma gave Tobias a small smile. "This is my son, Riley."

Cassidy patted Riley's head. "Later on, I'll bet Tobias will take you to the barn and show you the horses."

"Yay!"

She looked at Tobias. "Where's Deacon?"

He looked at her for a moment not quite comprehending the question. "Deacon? Oh, he's coming. We needed to take the calf away from his mother. Gonna have to try to hand feed him."

"Oh, poor thing. You're joining us for lunch, right?"

He turned his hat around in his hands. "Um...I should—"

"Come on. Ruthie made her enchilada casserole."

"Hmm. Can't turn that down, I guess." He glanced over his shoulder at the barn. "I need to put Chance away. And I'll wait for Deacon. Once we get the calf settled in, we'll come in to lunch."

"Okay. We'll wait for you."

Tobias made his escape. He couldn't believe the woman he'd met three days ago in a bar was here on his ranch. With her boyfriend. And her child. He took a deep breath. "Universe, you are a cruel, cruel bitch."

He unsaddled Chance and put him into his stall, then got an empty stall ready for the calf. It'd be touch and go whether the calf made it. But Tanner would take on the job of nursemaid. He was good at it, and he loved doing it. He'd saved more than one orphaned animal that shouldn't have survived. And Abby would be home tomorrow. She'd fill in if Tanner needed her to.

When Deacon rode into the barn with the calf draped over his saddle, Tobias lifted it down, and carried it to the stall. Deacon dismounted, and joined him.

"Poor guy."

"How'd the cow act when you rode off with him?"

"She didn't seem to care. Seems she was glad to be rid of him."

They watched the calf for a moment, then left him lying in the hay.

"I'll send Tanner out after lunch to look at him."

Deacon started unsaddling his horse. "Did Cassidy's friends arrive?"

"Yep."

Deacon glanced at him. "What?"

"Nothing."

Deacon pulled the saddle off and put it on the rack. "It's not nothing, brother. What's up?"

Tobias waited until Deacon put the horse away, then sighed. "The other night on my way back from Dallas, I stopped in Malady Springs for the night."

"Does it still smell like sulfur?"

"No." He frowned at Deacon. "Anyway. I found myself in the bar across the street from the hotel. I was going to have one drink, then call it a night."

"Okay."

"That was until this...woman. This incredible woman came into the bar."

Deacon nodded.

"She was beautiful and smart. Funny. Anyway, without going into too much detail, we parted the following morning, not knowing anything about each other."

"So you're never going to see this incredible woman again?"

"That's what I thought. Until about twenty minutes ago." He looked at Deacon. "She's currently in the house with Cassidy, her boyfriend, and her son."

"No shit."

"Definitely, shit."

"She's Cassidy's friend from college? Cassidy's maid of honor?"

"One and the same."

Deacon thought for a moment. "Isn't that a good thing? You get to see her again."

"Did you not hear the part about the boyfriend? And the child?"

"You like kids."

"Well, sure. But I'm not that fond of boyfriends."

"Right." Deacon folded his arms across his chest. "The way I see it, how invested could she be with this boyfriend if she spent the night with a complete stranger? Charming as he may be."

"I just don't get it. I didn't get the unavailable vibe from her at all."

"My point exactly."

"Yet here she is. At your wedding with her boyfriend, *Preston*."

Deacon laughed. "Be cool man. I don't want any drama at my wedding."

Tobias took a deep breath. "I'm cool. Don't worry. I'll simmer in silence."

Deacon patted Tobias on the shoulder. "Come on. Let's go eat lunch."

"Nah. I can't."

"You can't avoid her all week. You're my best man. I need you around."

"Fine. But only because you're my brother. And even though Cassidy chose the wrong Carmichael to marry, she deserves to have a drama-free wedding experience."

"There you go. That's the brother I know and love." They headed out of the barn. "So how incredible is this woman?"

"You know the whole fireworks thing?"

"Yeah."

"It was the friggin' Fourth of July, man."

Deacon put a hand on his shoulder. "Please be cool about this."

"I'm good. I'm cool."

Tobias and Deacon went into the house and found Cassidy and the others in the living room. Cassidy took Deacon's arm.

"And this is Deacon." She nodded toward Gemma. "This is Gemma, Preston, and Riley."

Deacon shook hands with all of them, including Riley, who was instantly enamored.

"Are you a real cowboy, too?"

Deacon glanced at Cassidy. "I'm afraid so."

"Cool. Do you have a horse and a gun?"

"I have a horse. But I don't generally carry a gun. Unless, of course, there are dangerous critters roaming around." Riley took his mother's hand, and Deacon added, "Tobias and I have scared them all away from the area, though. So you guys are safe." He smiled at Gemma. "Sorry. Didn't mean to put ideas into his head."

"It's fine. He's enchanted by all of this." She ventured a look at Tobias. "You guys have a beautiful home."

"Thank you." Deacon looked at Cassidy. "Where's my mother and Tanner?"

"Faith's in the kitchen with Ruthie, and Tanner's on the phone with Hallie."

"Of course."

Tobias was trying to melt into the background. Gemma looked beautiful. Her hair was down and wavy, and he just wanted to run his hands through it. *Stop.* Deacon glanced at him as though he could read what he was thinking.

Deacon cleared his throat. "So we brought the calf back. His mom didn't want anything to do with him."

Gemma looked concerned. "What will happen to him?"

"Our little brother, Tanner, will try to feed him." He glanced at Riley. "He's got about a fifty-fifty chance."

"Poor thing."

After lunch with an uncharacteristically quiet Tobias, Cassidy found Deacon in the barn watching Tanner feed the calf. She watched for a moment, then took Deacon's arm and led him outside.

"What's going on?"

"What do you mean?"

"Deacon. You know exactly what I mean. Tobias didn't say two words during lunch. Tobias. The life of the party."

"Oh. You noticed that, huh?"

"Of course I noticed it. Everyone was being weird. Even you. I felt like I was the only one not in on the secret."

He started walking, and she followed him. "It's not really my news to share, but since it involves your maid of honor, I suppose you should know."

"Know what?"

"He swears he won't let it interfere with the wedding."

"Oh my God, Deacon. Just tell me." Every possible and horrible scenario flashed through her mind.

He walked to one of the training pens and rested a foot on the bottom rail. "Seems Tobias and Gemma know each other."

"How?"

"Like *really* know each other."

"Intimately?"

Deacon nodded.

"How? And why would Gemma keep it from me?"

"She may very well be planning on telling you. But she wasn't expecting to see Tobias here. She didn't know he was your future brother-in-law."

"I'm really confused."

"They met a few days ago. At a bar in Malady Springs."

"Gemma was at a bar? This has to be a joke."

"I know when my brother's joking. He's totally freaked out she's here. Apparently, they had a *really* good time together. Like the Fourth of July, good time."

Cassidy walked a few feet away, then turned back to Deacon. "It doesn't make sense. She loves Preston. They're practically engaged. She wouldn't cheat on him."

"Maybe she's not as much in love as she pretends to be."

"She spent the night with Tobias and didn't tell him she had a boyfriend? It's so out of character."

Deacon shook his head. "They had a weird, no sharing personal information thing. He didn't even know her name."

"I can't believe this is happening."

Deacon went to her. "It's not happening to you. The ones who are suffering right now are Tobias and Gemma."

She hugged him. "Of course. You're right. No wonder lunch was so awkward." She looked at him. "What are we going to do about this?"

"*We* aren't going to do anything. If Gemma doesn't want to share this info with you, you need to act like you don't know anything."

"How am I supposed to do that?"

"Just chill."

She folded her arms across her chest. "Chill? That's your advice?"

"Yes."

"This is a nightmare."

"Only if we let it become one."

Cassidy frowned at him. "Quit being so pragmatic."

"You like that I'm pragmatic."

"Not in this case. I want you to be as panicked about this as I am."

"I'm not going to panic over Tobias' one night stand. I don't care how big the fireworks were."

Chapter Three

"So, I have a confession to make."

Tobias was rubbing down a saddle in the barn. He had to do something to stay busy and keep away from the house. If he were Deacon in this situation, he'd be cleaning out stalls.

"So you went to Yale, huh?"

He turned around to find Gemma a few feet away. "And you have a son. And a *boyfriend*." He set the rag he was using and the can of saddle soap aside and picked up the saddle. He walked by her and set the saddle on a rack, before turning back to her and shrugging. "It's my own damn fault. No personal information. At the time, it seemed fun and mysterious. Now. It kind of sucks."

She took a step toward him and he backed up two. She put up a hand. "Let me explain."

"No need. You thought you'd never see me again. I get it." He put his hands in his pockets and tried not to think about how good it was to see her. Regardless of the boyfriend situation.

"No. You don't. I don't want you to think I cheated on Preston."

"But you did. With me. Do you have a thing for cowboys, or will any man do?"

She closed the gap between them and slapped him, then took a step back and put a hand to her mouth.

Tobias rubbed his cheek. "I guess I deserved that."

She took a moment to collect herself. "What happened in Malady Springs was... I don't do that. I'm not what you think I am."

"What are you, Gemma? Tell me. Now that we no longer need to keep up the 'no personal information' game, tell me what you are."

She sighed, then sat on a wooden bench. "Preston and I haven't been together for six months."

"Yet you're here at my brother's wedding, introducing him as your boyfriend."

"It's complicated."

"I'm sure it is." He started to walk away.

"Wait. Please."

Tobias stopped and looked at her. "I haven't been able to get you out of my head. For the last three days, you're all I could think about. But apparently to you, I was just a one-night stand."

She shook her head. "No. It wasn't like that. I swear. That's not what it was. When I said no regrets, I meant it. What we had that night was..."

Tobias sighed. "Let's just try to forget about it. Don't worry about me spilling the beans. That's not who *I* am. This is my brother's wedding. And I'm not going to let anything, including you, do anything to ruin it." He took a few steps, then stopped. "Just stay away from me. That's all I ask."

As he left the barn, Cassidy was coming in. "Oh, hey." She looked at him. "Are you okay?"

"I've got to go check on the horses in the paddock."

"Okay. Dinner's at seven."

He nodded and walked away.

⁂

Gemma was still on the bench when Cassidy came into the barn. She walked up to her and held out her hand. "Let's go take a walk."

Gemma looked at her and nodded as she took Cassidy's hand. They left the barn and headed down the driveway. "Deacon said I shouldn't say anything, but I need to. I know about your night in Malady Springs."

Gemma stopped walking. "How does Deacon know?"

"Tobias told him."

"Oh, my gosh. You all must think I'm a horrible person."

"No. I don't. I just don't understand."

"I didn't cheat on Preston." They stopped at a bench under an oak tree and sat down. "I guess technically I did. But we haven't been a couple in six months."

"What happened?"

"He wasn't who I wanted to spend the rest of my life with. I don't love him. And I don't think I ever did."

"Okay. So why are you here with him?"

"Riley. Riley loves him. And Preston is really good with him. I haven't figured out how to end that relationship."

"They could still see each other. You and Preston get along. Right?"

"Yes. He moved out five months ago. We told Riley it was because of work. But when we got the invite to your wedding, Riley was so excited to come and share this experience with Preston. I couldn't bring myself to not invite him."

Cassidy stood and walked a few feet away. "So, awkward question. Where were Preston and Riley the other night when you were with Tobias?"

"We came in separate cars. Preston had to work until Friday and Riley had school. I wanted to leave on Friday and unwind before I got here. So I rented a car. They left Saturday, and we met in Connelly last night." She looked at the ground for a few moments, then back at Cassidy. "Dammit, I really like Tobias. That night was..." She sighed. "You know me. I don't sleep with random guys."

Cassidy returned to the bench and took Gemma's hand. "I'm about to marry a Carmichael. Believe me, I know all about the masculine charisma they exude. It's hard to ignore. And just so all my cards are on the table, I dated Tobias briefly."

Gemma turned and looked at her. "You did?"

"Yes. I wouldn't even call it dating. We hung out. He's very sweet. And he's a good man."

"Did you...?"

"No. We never even got close to that. My heart belonged to Deacon, even then. Tobias and I never had a chance."

"Does Deacon know?"

"Oh, yeah. Everybody knows. It was messy briefly. The other thing the Carmichael brothers possess is a heavy dose of loyalty and honor."

"Maybe it's best that it started and ended in Malady Springs."

"If you're not ready to give up your life and move to Connelly, please steer clear of Tobias, and don't start anything with him. He means a lot to me. He's family."

"I understand. Don't worry. I'm pretty sure he hates me, anyway."

"Tobias can be moody, and he strikes out when he's upset. But I'm sure he doesn't hate you."

"I'll steer clear of him, as he asked. And I won't let any of this affect your wedding. I promise."

"I'd appreciate that."

Cassidy was in the bathroom getting ready for dinner when Deacon appeared in the doorway. She gave him a smile.

"I'll be done in a minute."

"Take your time. I'm just enjoying the view."

She moved to him and put her arms around his neck. He hugged her and pulled her in for a kiss. "Will you still enjoy the view when I'm old and overweight, with gray hair and wrinkles?"

"Of course. I'll be even older, with no hair and more wrinkles than you. It's hard for a working cowboy to get overweight, though, so I'll be lean and mean."

"A sexy mature cowboy. I think I'll be okay with that." She let go of him and left the bathroom. "So, I have a confession to make."

Deacon sat on the edge of the bed. "Let me guess. You talked to Gemma about Tobias."

She put her hands on her hips. "How'd you know?"

"I know you. And I knew you wouldn't be able to let it go."

She went to the bed and sat next to him. "I had to hear her side of things."

"And?"

"She and Preston broke up six months ago."

"So why the hell—"

"Because of Riley. She's trying to protect Riley from losing the first father figure he's had."

Deacon took her hand. "Hmm. That's rough, I guess. Poor kid."

"He's really cute though, isn't he?"

Deacon let go of her hand and got to his feet. "Don't start."

"You said we'd talk about it before we got married. You're running out of time."

"Do you really want to have this conversation now while there are guest waiting downstairs for dinner?"

Cassidy got to her feet and walked to him. She took his hands in hers. "I'm just giving you a hard time. We'll have the conversation when you're ready to have it. No pressure. I promise."

"It's not that I don't want kids someday."

"I know." She hugged him. "Let's go downstairs."

"I just need to use the bathroom. Someone's been hogging it for the last hour."

"I haven't even been up here for an hour. Go. It's all yours. I'll be downstairs."

Deacon watched her go, then sat on the bed again. He knew she wanted to have kids. Plural. Lots of them. And the idea of it didn't completely freak him out. But they'd only been together for seven months. They rushed into the marriage, which felt right. But the kid thing, he didn't want to rush into that. She thought he just wasn't ready to talk about it. He was hesitant to tell her the real reason. His father dying and leaving behind a wife and a family had left a deep scar that would never heal. Could he really take the chance of doing that to his own kids? His father's death was an accident. But it could happen to anyone. Deacon spent a lot of time on horses. Who's to say he might not someday be kicked in the head by an ornery one? Did he have the right to take away Cassidy's desire for children because of his fear? Probably not.

He went to splash some water on his face to clear his head, then left the room and headed down the hall. On a hunch, he stopped at

Tobias' door and knocked. When he didn't get an answer, he open it. Tobias was on the couch with a glass in his hand. A bottle of rum was on the table next to him.

Deacon entered the room and closed the door. "What the hell are you doing?"

"Sorry. I can't go sit at dinner with her. Not tonight. I'll be fine tomorrow, I promise."

Deacon looked at the bottle, which was half-empty. "How much of that did you drink?"

Tobias shrugged. "It was already opened. Not all of it."

Deacon picked it up. "I'll take this with me."

Tobias scowled at him. "Dammit. Just let me have tonight."

"No. You need to get the Arabian ready for Abby. You promised you'd have him saddle broke for her when she came home. You dragged your ass and now she'll be here tomorrow."

"I've been working with him. He's broke. Just a little skittish still. Nothing Abby can't handle."

"We're not sending her out riding on a skittish horse. Work with him tomorrow. Take him out on the trail. You can't do that if you're hungover."

"Yes, sir. Whatever you say."

"Don't be an ass. You know I'm right."

Tobias nodded. "Give my apologies to your guests. Tell them... Tell them whatever the hell you want to tell them. I don't really care."

Deacon studied him for a moment. "Why are you so upset about this woman? It was one night."

Tobias looked at him. "The fireworks man. The damn fireworks."

Chapter Four

"That's a lot of maybes."

Deacon left Tobias' room with the bottle of rum. He went down the stairs and found everyone passing by on their way to the dining room. He smiled at Cassidy as he put the bottle behind his back. She ushered everyone toward the dining room, before going to him.

He held up the bottle. "Tobias won't be joining us."

"Is he drunk?"

"No. And he won't be unless he has another bottle stashed in his room. I'll go put this away and join you in a minute."

She kissed him. "Okay." She smiled. "This is me trying not to panic."

He winked at her. "You're doing a hell of a job."

She continued to the dining room and Deacon took the bottle to the den and put it behind the bar. Before he left, he poured himself a half shot of scotch and drank it down. He didn't like having guests in the house. He liked his privacy. He liked family dinner with just the family. He looked at the bottle of scotch, then sighed. One slightly drunk Carmichael was enough.

When he entered the dining room, Faith was asking Gemma what she thought of the ranch. It seemed Mother was mentally present this evening and was playing the role of hostess. Deacon took his seat next to Cassidy and Faith looked at him. "Where's your brother?"

He glanced at Tanner, but decided he probably shouldn't make light of the situation. "Tobias is a bit under the weather, Mother."

"Oh dear. Nothing serious, I hope." Tobias' drinking was another thing she chose not to acknowledge.

"He should be fine tomorrow."

"Good. We don't want anything to interfere with the wedding." She looked at Gemma and Preston. "I've waited a long time for Deacon to find the right woman." She smiled at Cassidy. "It seems it was worth the wait."

Cassidy returned her smile. "Thank you, Faith. That means a lot."

"Of course, dear. Now don't make me wait too long for grandchildren."

Deacon cleared his throat and nodded at Ruthie, who was standing in the doorway with a tray. She came in and served everyone a salad.

Preston looked at Deacon. "So, this is quite the ranch. What's your main stream of income?"

"Um... We have several, really. But cattle makes up the bulk of it." He really didn't want to discuss the family business with a stranger.

"Interesting. You seem to have quite a few horses, too."

"Yes. We buy and sell horses. Do some breeding and some training. Tanner is our horse whisperer. He's quite good in the training pen."

"I'm in finance and I'm aware of what it costs to keep a place this large going."

Cassidy smiled at Riley. "Have you seen the horses yet?"

"No. Mom won't let me go there alone."

"I'm sorry no one took you to the barn today. We'll make sure you get the tour tomorrow. We've got more than just horses. There's lots to see."

Riley smiled. "Cool." He looked at Tanner. "Can you show me how to whisper to a horse?"

Tanner laughed. "Sure. But it's more of a mind meld."

"Cool!"

Deacon glanced at Cassidy and gave her a 'thank you for changing the subject' smile. She reached over and patted his knee.

"So tomorrow you get to meet Abby. She's been away at college." Cassidy glanced at Deacon. "She's very happy to be coming home for the summer."

Deacon nodded. "She's missed the ranch."

Faith smiled. "I believe she's missed her brothers, too."

They managed to get through dinner without Preston asking anymore prying questions, and everyone retired early. Tomorrow would be a big day. Abby would be home in the early afternoon, and there was a barbecue planned for a few close friends and family.

When Cassidy and Deacon went upstairs and passed Tobias' room, she stopped outside the door. "I want to talk to him for a moment."

"Alone?"

"Yeah."

"Okay. Don't let him sweet-talk you into fetching his bottle of rum."

"Don't worry. I don't want him hungover tomorrow even more than you don't."

"I'll see you soon." Deacon continued to the room.

Tobias was snoozing on the couch when he heard the knock on his door. He sat up.

"Unless you're bringing me back my bottle of rum, go away."

Cassidy opened the door. "It's me. And no rum. Are you decent?"

"I'm so much more than decent. Unfortunately, you'll never get the chance to find out."

"Tobias, behave. I just want to talk."

He waved her in. "I'll always talk to you. You're my favorite sister-in-law."

She went to the couch and sat next to him. "I'm sorry about Gemma."

He scowled at her. "You know about Gemma? Of course you do. Deacon tells you everything."

"I talked to her about it. I wanted to get her side of it."

"I'm sure she had a lot to say."

"She's not with Preston. And hasn't been for a while."

"So she says."

"I believe her. I've known her for seven years. We roomed together for three. She had to leave the dorm when she had Riley. And she moved in with her family until she graduated. Gemma is a good person and a good mother. She doesn't make a habit of meeting guys in bars."

"So, I just got lucky? Her one night of slumming she runs into me?"

"She wouldn't have spent time with you if she didn't see what I see in you."

"What's that? It's certainly not what you see in Deacon."

"A good man. A caring man. And a pretty darn funny man, when he's not feeling sorry for himself."

He rearranged the pillow behind his back. "I'm not feeling sorry for myself."

"You kind of are."

He took a moment, then sighed. "I just really, *really* had a good time. And I was okay knowing it was a one-time thing. That I'd never see her again. It allowed me to envision her anyway I wanted to. But suddenly, she's here. On the ranch. With a *boyfriend* and a kid. It burst the bubble."

"I understand."

"She took away my fantasy and smacked me in the face with reality."

Cassidy took his hand. "Well, maybe you should take the time to get to know who Gemma really is."

"To what end? In a week, she'll be gone. With her *boyfriend* and her son. Back to wherever she came from. And I'll still never see her again."

"Maybe the reality will look better by then. Maybe it'll be easier to live with." She held up a finger. "*Maybe* you'll like the real Gemma and it'll improve the fantasy."

Tobias shook his head. "That's a lot of maybes."

"Maybe so."

"You know I wouldn't be in this mess if you'd just fallen for me instead of Deacon. I never would've gone to the bar. I would've been in the hotel—"

"Okay. Let's not pursue that fantasy."

He grinned. "Okay, sister-in-law."

She let go of his hand and patted his arm. "You know I love you." He raised an eyebrow, and she added, "Like a brother."

He turned and looked at her. "I kid around about it, but I'm really happy for you and Deacon. You were obviously meant to be together."

Cassidy moved closer and hugged him. "You'll find your someone. You're young. You have a lot of time to find the perfect woman."

"I am young. A lot younger than the old man you're about to marry."

Cassidy laughed. "Yeah. He's not as old as you think."

Tobias put his hands over his ears. "No, no, no. I don't want to hear that. I'm still carrying a tiny little torch for you. I don't want to hear how virile my brother is. The glimpse of the salacious kiss in the classroom was more than enough."

"So, you're going to be alright? You can get back to 'the life of the party', Tobias?"

"I'll do my best to make you laugh throughout this week of festivities."

"Thank you. I'm counting on it."

The two guest rooms were set up with a shared bathroom between them. When Preston came into Gemma's room and sat on the bed, she cocked her head at him.

"Don't get too comfortable."

"Don't worry. I just can't go to sleep at eight o'clock. And Riley's in bed." Preston would be spending the night with Riley, not her. But he was right. It was early.

She thought for a moment. "Rummy?"

He smiled. "Did you bring cards?"

Gemma pulled a deck of cards from her bag. "I never go any-where without them."

Preston moved to a small table with two chairs and Gemma sat across from him. She shuffled the cards, before dealing them.

While he rearranged his cards, he looked over them at Gemma. "What's with Tobias?"

She looked at him. "What do you mean?"

"He seems a little stand-offish."

"Deacon said he wasn't feeling well."

"That sounded like an excuse. I think he doesn't like me for some reason."

Of course, Preston would assume it was about him. In a way, it kind of was. "You barely spent any time with him. I'm sure he'll be fine tomorrow. Cassidy says he's quite personable."

"Hmm. We'll see, I guess." He looked around the room. "This is quite the place, though. These guys are loaded. Your friend did pretty well for herself."

"Preston, don't be an ass. Cassidy couldn't care less about the money."

"Still. She hit the jackpot. And they only met, what? Like six or seven months ago?"

"And your point?"

"Just seems fast."

"Well, sometimes, when you know, you know." Her mind went to her night in Malady Springs. She didn't believe in love at first sight. But if she did, that night would've been just that.

"Are you going to make a move, or what?"

"What? Oh. Yes." She drew a card and discarded one from her hand. What would've happened if she'd shown up without Preston?

How would Tobias have reacted then? She didn't think he had a problem with Riley.

"Yo. Gem. Get your mind in the game."

They played for two hours and Gemma managed to keep her mind off of Tobias. But at ten, she told Preston she was ready to go to bed.

He stood and stretched. "Okay. Big barbecue tomorrow."

"Cassidy says we'll be eating Carmichael beef."

"Great. Probably freshly butchered. I don't care how much money they have. There's something barbaric about that."

"I'm sure they don't butcher the cows themselves."

"Of course not. They have someone else do the dirty work for them."

She gathered the cards and stashed them in the box. "What's the difference between eating fresh beef here, and supposedly fresh beef in your favorite restaurant?"

"In my favorite restaurant, I can't see the cows out the window."

She cocked her head at him. "Goodnight, Preston."

"I'm sharing a bed with a six-year-old. It's probably not going to be a good night."

He left and Gemma got ready for bed, then climbed under the covers. She looked at the ceiling and wondered what Tobias was doing right now. Was he sleeping soundly? Or was he up there thinking about her?

She rolled onto her side. He was probably up there wishing they'd never run into each other in Malady Springs.

Chapter Five

"For a huge ranch, it's surprisingly small."

Tobias was in the round training pen with the Arabian. Abby would be home in a few hours. He really wanted her to be able to ride the horse if she wanted to. Deacon was right. He had been dragging his feet. They'd gotten the horse in the fall, and here is was May and he was barely ridable. Tobias' only excuse was he'd paid way too much for the horse who was average at best and had a stubborn streak he couldn't seem to break through. It was easier just to write him off and take the loss, rather than accept responsibility for buying him when he was mad at Deacon.

He was riding around the edge of the ring when he spotted Riley running toward the pen, with Gemma not far behind. Tobias stopped the horse on the far side of the pen.

Riley reached the fence and peered through the rails, as Gemma came up behind him. Tobias crossed the pen to them.

Gemma looked up at him. "I'm sorry. He saw you and I wasn't quick enough."

"It's fine." He walked the horse close enough for Riley to pet him. "Go ahead. Give him a pat on the nose. Just move slowly. If you spook him, I'm likely to end up on the ground."

Riley laughed, then gently rubbed the horse's nose. "What's his name?"

"Aladdin. He's my sister's horse."

"Like the movie?"

"Um..." Tobias looked at Gemma and she nodded. "Yeah. Exactly. Like the movie."

"I like him."

"Yeah, he's pretty cool. He's not so sure about wearing a saddle."

"What else would he wear?"

Tobias laughed. "A suit? A bathrobe?"

Riley started laughing uncontrollably, and Aladdin got nervous. Tobias backed him up a few feet.

Gemma looked at him again. "Sorry."

"It's fine. I need to take Aladdin for a short ride and see how he does outside of this pen. But when I get back, I'll take you in the barn and introduce you to all the horses."

Riley jumped up and down. "Yay!"

"In the meantime. If you and your mom go around the side of the barn, you'll find some chickens, ducks, and geese. And just past them, the goats and the sheep. There's even a couple of llamas back there. But steer clear of them. They're a little ornery."

"Cool, Mom, can we go?"

"Yes, honey." She looked up at Tobias and mouthed, "Thank you."

He tipped his hat and walked Aladdin to the gate.

As Gemma took Riley's hand and headed for the side of the barn, she watched Tobias ride off across the field. He was definitely a cowboy. She'd never had a feeling one way or the other about cowboys. Anyone who wore a cowboy hat and boots in Austin, weren't really cowboys. Not like Tobias and his brothers. She had a whole new perspective of what the title meant. And she found it quite interesting and attractive.

She spent an hour with Riley checking out all the animals. As Tobias had promised, there were a lot of them. It was like their very own petting zoo. Riley seemed to be fascinated by the chickens, entertained by the goats, and intimidated by the llamas. After a while, Tanner joined them.

"I thought you two might be out here." He pulled up a handful of grass and handed it to Riley. "You can feed them."

"Cool!"

Gemma watched the goats eat from Riley's hand. "Tobias steered us over here."

Tanner nodded. "Yeah, I thought he was in the training pen."

"He was. He took off that way about an hour ago."

"He wants to make sure Aladdin is ready for Abby. It's her new horse. Or newest horse. We've had him since last fall, but she's been gone since January."

"At school, right?"

He pulled some more grass and handed it to Riley. "Yeah. Southwestern. She got lucky. She was able to talk Deacon into letting her stay close. Plus, she got to hold off for two and a half years."

"You look like you're about ready to head off to college."

Tanner shrugged. "Yeah. One more year, then Yale."

"Impressive."

He frowned. "It's the family legacy."

"Deacon and Tobias both went to Yale?"

"Yeah."

"You don't sound that excited."

Tanner smiled. "I'm not."

"It's pretty far away."

"Exactly. And no horses."

"That's very true."

Riley came up to them. "Can I see the horses now?"

Tanner looked down at him. "Sure I can take you." He glanced at Gemma. "Is it okay?"

"Yes, of course. Tobias was going to take him in when he got back. But I'm sure he has better things to do."

Tanner took Riley's hand. "Come on. I'll introduce you to everyone."

Gemma followed them, then stopped when she saw Tobias headed back. She waited outside the barn for him. He rode up, then stopped the horse and dismounted with a slight grunt.

She watched him for a moment as he tied the horse to a post.

"When did you hurt your leg?"

He looked at her. "Excuse me?"

"I can tell how you move. You favor your left leg. But not like it's a new injury. It's something you've been living with."

"You can tell by watching me get off a horse."

"And walk. It's not overtly obvious. I just notice those things."

He took his gloves off and tucked them in his pocket. Then remove his hat and hung it on the saddle horn. "Six years ago. My horse hit the rail on a jump and we both went down. She rolled over me and broke my leg in a couple places."

"Goodness. I'm sorry. And it still bothers you?"

"Now and then."

"I don't quite believe that."

He folded his arms across his chest. "Fine. It hurts all the time. But most of the time, I can deal with it."

"And when you can't?"

He shook his head. "Why do you care?"

"It's what I do. I'm a physical therapist. I work with athletes who are injured while playing."

Tobias laughed. "That's a far cry from CEO for an accounting firm in San Antonio."

"Maybe. But much more fulfilling."

"I suppose."

"So, what do you do for pain management?"

He put his hat back on and untied Aladdin. "I don't need you diagnosing me. I spent plenty of time and money on doctors, pain management, and physical therapy. I even saw a shrink. I'm done with all that." He headed for the barn.

"You seem too clear-headed to be on narcotic pain relievers."

He stopped and looked at her. "I haven't taken narcotics since I left the hospital."

"So you're just toughing it out."

"Again. Why do you care?"

"Maybe I can help you."

He started moving again. "I don't need your help. Honestly, I don't want your help." He stopped once more and looked at her. "But if you must know. Rum. Rum is my go to pain reliever." He walked away and went into the barn.

She followed him, and he glanced back and frowned. "Gemma, I don't want to talk about this."

She raised a hand. "I know. I'm just joining Tanner and Riley."

He nodded as she passed by. "You're not doing a very good job."

She stopped. "At what?"

"Staying away from me."

"For a huge ranch, it's surprisingly small."

He almost smiled. "At the barbecue, stay on the other side of the yard."

"Okay."

Riley and Tanner were at the other end of the barn, and when Riley laughed, Gemma and Tobias both looked at him.

"He seems like a decent kid."

"Decent?"

"Good, cool, whatever."

"Thank you."

"I've got to put my horse away."

"Right. And I've got to keep my distance."

Tobias busied himself with putting away Aladdin, but while doing so, he was listening to Gemma and Tanner talk. He shook his head. *Pain management? I do just fine, thank you very much.*

When he left the barn, he saw Deacon getting into his Cherokee. Tobias whistled, and Deacon stopped and looked at him.

"Hold up." Tobias joined Deacon at the vehicle. "Are you going to get Abby?"

"Yeah. She should be getting into town real soon. I'm picking her up at the rental car place."

"I'll come with."

"Okay." They both got into the Jeep. Then Deacon looked at Tobias. "Why do you want to come with me all of a sudden?"

"I like Abby. I missed her."

"Right. And the fact Gemma and Riley are in the barn has nothing to do with your sudden interest in driving into town with me."

"Nope. Not at all. I told you, I can handle it."

"Hmm." Deacon turned over the ignition, then headed down the driveway. "So, I saw you two talking a little while ago."

Tobias shrugged. "Seems she's in tune to injuries."

"Oh, right. She's some kind of therapist. She works at the University of Austin with the football team, I believe."

"Seriously?"

"Yeah. She must know what she's talking about."

"Well, good for her."

Deacon shook his head. "It couldn't hurt to see what she has to say."

"Not interested."

"You're a stubborn bastard, you know that?"

"It takes one to know one."

They drove the rest of the way in silence and when they pulled into the rental car office, Abby was standing outside with two suitcases. She waved when she saw them. Deacon pulled up next to her, and both men got out of the car.

Abby hugged Deacon and then Tobias. "Oh my gosh, I missed you guys."

Tobias put his arm around her. "Not as much as we missed you."

"That's not even possible." She took a deep breath. "Clean air. I love it."

Tobias put her suitcases in the back of the Jeep, then opened the passenger door for her. "I'll even let you sit in the front."

"Oh, wow. What a privilege."

Deacon looked at her. "Have you eaten? Are you hungry?"

"I just want to go home."

"Home it is."

They drove out of town and headed toward home on the small two-lane highway. Abby looked back at Tobias. "Has Cassidy's friend arrived yet?"

"Why are you asking me?"

Deacon cleared his throat. "Yes. She got to the ranch yesterday."

Abby looked at him, then back at Tobias. "What am I missing? What's going on?"

Deacon looked at Tobias through the rearview mirror. Tobias shrugged. "Whatever. She'll find out sooner or later."

Deacon glanced at Abby. "Seems our brother and Cassidy's friend had a...thing a few nights ago."

"A thing?" She looked at Tobias. "A thing? She just got here."

Deacon went on. "They met in Malady Springs a couple of nights ago. And ah...connected."

Abby turned in her seat and frowned at Tobias. "Why would you do that?"

Tobias shrugged.

Deacon laughed. "In his defense, if there is one, he didn't know who she was. They didn't exchange any information. They apparently shared a few other things, but—"

Tobias thumped Deacon on the back of the head.

Abby looked at him again. "Hold on. Let me get this straight. You and Cassidy's friend meet up, accidentally. Hook up. Then part, not knowing you're going to see each other in a few days?"

Tobias nodded. "Judge me all you want. It was totally worth it."

"I'm not judging. It's so coincidental. But now you get to see her again. That's great."

Deacon shook his head. "Not really great. She came with her son." He glanced at Tobias through the mirror again. "And her boyfriend."

"Oh shit." Abby covered her mouth. "Sorry. That's what sending me to college did." She turned around and looked at Tobias again. "She cheated on her boyfriend with you?"

He scowled. "Technically, no. I didn't know she had a boyfriend. I didn't know anything about her. And now she's saying she and *Preston* aren't actually together."

"And you believe her?"

He shrugged again.

Deacon spoke up. "I believe her. Cassidy says, that's not who Gemma is."

Abby released her seat belt.

"What are you doing?"

"My brother needs a hug." She climbed through the space between the seats and sat next to Tobias.

"I'm fine. I don't need—"

Abby put her arms around him. "Of course you do."

Tobias gave into the hug. He had to admit. He did kind of need one right about now.

Chapter Six

Was this thing walking around yesterday?"

T he barbecue was in full swing. Half the guests were relatives, and the other half were close friends, with the total count close to thirty people. Tobias was trying to lie low by helping the men who were manning the giant barbecue. It was a four-by-six foot grill heated with propane and it currently had twenty-five prime Carmichael-bred steaks cooking on it. One end of it was dedicated to hamburgers for the kids or the adults who didn't want steak. But this was cattle country. If you didn't like steak, you were in the wrong place.

Cassidy came up to Tobias with a beer and she handed it to him. "You're taking over Deacon's job."

"How so? I thought his job was to be your escort."

"That's true. It is. But you know he can't help making sure every-one is doing their job and everything is running smoothly."

Tobias took a sip of the beer. "And I'm interfering with that?"

"A little bit, yes." She smiled. "So, thank you."

"He should have nothing on his mind but you."

She kissed him on the cheek. "You're very sweet, Tobias."

"I've been telling you, you're marrying the wrong brother."

She spotted Gemma talking across the yard. "How goes it with you and my maid of honor?"

Tobias laughed. "She's keeping her distance as I asked her to do."

"Tobias. You need to give her a chance."

"For what? Even if the whole boyfriend thing is non-existent. She still lives in Austin. And apparently has a pretty cool job there. So I know a dead-end when I see it."

"That doesn't mean you can't be friends while she's here."

"I don't want to be her friend. You can't go from...where we went then backtrack into the friend zone."

"So, be more than friends, then."

"Miss O'Hare. What are you suggesting?"

"I'm suggesting you only live once. If you want to spend time with her while she's here. Spend time with her."

"With her boyfriend looking on? Maybe we could ask him to join us. But I don't really roll that way." He drank some more beer.

"Tobias. Obviously, some discretion would be involved."

He shook his head. "I can't believe you're suggesting what you're suggesting."

She shrugged. "Since I met Deacon I've changed my attitude toward fate and missed opportunities."

"Really? Are you sorry you wasted your time with me and didn't go right for the prize?"

"Not at all. I loved the time we spent together."

"Hmm."

"Really. That's why I understand how Gemma went for the gold a few hours after she met you."

"Gold, huh? Why didn't you?"

"Because you weren't my treasure. But apparently you're hers."

He studied the label on his beer bottle. "It's hard enough not thinking about that one night. Adding a few more to it won't make it any easier."

Cassidy sighed. "Okay."

"Why does your 'okay' sound like 'you're an idiot?'"

She patted his cheek. "If the shoe fits."

She wandered off and Tobias made his way to Deacon, who was talking with Ruthie. From the look on her face, he was trying to micro-manage her.

"I've been serving food at family barbecues for more years than you've lived. So you watch your tone, young man."

Tobias came up behind Deacon and put a hand on his shoulder. "Please don't make the cook mad, brother."

Deacon glanced at him. "I was merely suggesting—"

He stopped when Ruthie pointed a finger at him.

Tobias smiled at Ruthie. "I'll get him out of your hair."

"Thank you, honey."

Tobias took Deacon's arm and started him walking away from Ruthie. "So now I'm her honey and you're the troublemaker. How'd that happen?"

"Don't worry, she'll soon realize her mistake."

They stopped walking and Tobias let go of Deacon's arm. "Shouldn't you be with your lovely fiancé?"

"Where the hell is she, anyway?"

Tobias looked around. "She probably ran off with Preston. Apparently he's available."

Deacon took the beer from Tobias' hand and took a drink. "So you've accepted the fact he and Gemma aren't together?"

"Yes."

"So, what are you going to do about that?"

Tobias laughed. "Not you, too."

"Not me too, what?"

"Cassidy just suggested I make the most of Gemma's time here."

"It's not a terrible idea."

Tobias shook his head. "Of course it's a terrible idea. I'm not going to start something with someone who lives halfway across the great state of Texas."

"Seems to me you already did."

"Yeah. But I didn't know she lived in Austin at the time. I didn't care where she lived."

Deacon finished off Tobias' beer. "Exactly. So why do you care now?"

"I feel like I'm in some alternate universe where I'm the voice of reason."

Deacon laughed. "I just want you to be happy. That's all."

"Well, hooking up with Gemma again, only to see her walk out the door again, won't make me happy."

"Okay. I understand." He handed the empty beer bottle to Tobias. "I need to go find Cassidy before she takes off with Preston."

Tobias handed the bottle to a passing server, then wandered away from the party and went to the barn. He and his siblings always found solace in a barn full of horses. It was familiar and comforting. He went to Chase's stall, and the horse came up to him.

"Hey, buddy. Quite the shindig going on out there."

When a few pieces of hay dropped down on him from the hayloft over his head, Tobias looked up, then grinned when he heard some movement. He wasn't positive, but he was pretty sure it was Tanner and his girlfriend, Hallie. He gave Chase one last pat, then headed out of the barn. As he left, he met Hallie's twin sister coming through the door.

"Oh, hey. Hester, right?"

"Yeah. Have you seen my sister?"

"Um...no." He glanced over his shoulder. "There's no one in the barn."

"Okay." She sighed. "She and Tanner kind of abandoned me."

"Sorry. Looks like we're about to eat though. So if you'll do me the honor, I don't have anyone to eat with. If you don't mind hanging out with an old guy, that is."

She blushed. "You know everyone here."

"Sure. But they're all hanging out together. They kind of abandoned me."

He bent his arm and offered it to her. After a moment's hesitation, she took it. "Thank you."

"My pleasure."

———————————

Hallie giggled and Tanner shushed her as she whispered, "We almost got caught."

"Tobias is cool. He wouldn't have said anything." He leaned in and kissed her.

Hallie pulled away from him. "I think it's about time to eat."

He grinned. "I am kind of hungry." He kissed her again.

"Stop."

Tanner moved away from her. "Fine. Sorry."

"It's okay. But you know I'm not ready to go down that road."

"Of course. I'd never—"

"I know. Because you're a sweet boy. You're the sweetest boy I've ever dated."

Tanner wasn't sure if that was necessarily a good thing. But he knew for sure he didn't want to tell her she was the only girl he'd ever dated. He'd had a couple of one date relationships. But he'd had his eye on her since sophomore year.

"We should go." He stood and held out his hand to her. She took it and he pulled her to her feet.

She smiled. "How many girls have you brought up to the hayloft?"

"You're the first."

She kissed him on the cheek. "So sweet."

They climbed down the ladder, then headed for the door. As they were going out, Abby was coming in.

She stopped and smiled at them. "Oh, hey."

"Hi, Abby."

Abby glanced at Hallie, then picked some hay out of Tanner's hair. "Enjoying the barbecue?"

Tanner blushed. "We were just..."

She put a hand on his arm. "Don't worry. I was seventeen once."

"You make it sound like it was so long ago."

"Once you go to college, seventeen is a lifetime ago."

He stepped away from her. "Right. We're gonna go eat."

"I'll be there in a minute."

Abby went to Aladdin's stall and stroked his nose. "So what's this I hear about you being stubborn?"

"It's because he's a damn Arabian."

Abby turned to see Skyler approaching. She ran to him and gave him a hug. "You're here."

"Of course. Do you think I'm not good enough to be invited to a Carmichael barbecue?"

"Oh, my God. It's so good to see you." She stood back and looked at him. Is it possible he'd gotten better looking over the last five months?

He gave her one of his beautiful smiles. "How you doing, Abby?"

"I'm extremely glad to be home." She turned back to Aladdin. She and Skyler had been friends since they met at the gala. But after not seeing him for a while, she'd forgotten just how good looking he was. She didn't want that to cloud her judgement.

"Are you back for the summer?"

"Yes. I took my exams early."

He looked at her. "What's wrong?"

He'd always been able to read her. "I hate it. I mean, I *really* hate it."

"I'm sorry. It's your first semester. It'll grow on you."

"I don't think so. I'm just wasting my time. I want to be home with my family and my horses." She turned back to him and took his hand. "And my friends. I really missed you."

"I missed you too."

She pulled him down onto a bench. "What have you been up to? Tell me everything."

"Well, my parents have gotten into their heads that it's time for me to get married."

"No way. You're only twenty-three."

"I know."

She'd never liked his parents. Even before she got to know Skyler. They were part of the pretentious rich rancher group she hated. "So they're bugging you to find a wife?"

"No, they've decided they'll find one for me."

She was astounded. "Skyler. No. You can't let them do that to you."

"They say it's my obligation to marry. And to marry the right woman."

"Is this Victorian England?"

"Apparently it is at the Fremont Ranch."

She shook her head. "You have to fight it."

"Well, I think fighting it would be equal to a mutiny. I'm pretty sure they'd disown me."

"They can't disown you. You're their only son. You're the heir to the family fortune."

He shrugged. "That doesn't mean they can't threaten to give it all away to someone else."

"This is very distressing news. We need to find you a wife before they do."

He raised an eyebrow. "You want to help find me a wife?"

"If it will save you from an arranged marriage or disinheritance, yes."

He kissed her on the cheek. "You're a good friend, Abby." He stood. "Let's go get some steak."

"This discussion isn't over."

"Let's save it for another day."

Tobias and Hester were sitting at one of the long tables near the end. When Gemma, Riley, and Preston came to the table, the only available seats were the ones directly in front of Tobias and Hester.

Gemma looked at Tobias, and he cocked his head, then said, "Have a seat."

She nodded and sat across from him, with Riley on one side and Preston on the other.

Preston looked at Tobias. "This is quite the feast."

"We do it right, here in rural Texas."

"Yeah. I guess you do." When a server plopped a steak down on Preston's plate, he studied it for a moment. "Was this thing walking around yesterday?"

Tobias grinned. "I believe it was."

Gemma smiled as a steak was put on her plate, then looked at the young man serving as she nodded toward Riley. "A burger for this guy."

Riley was served a huge burger, which seemed to delight him and Tobias grinned.

"Are you going to be able to eat all of that?"

Riley shrugged. "I don't know."

The rest of the food was set out family style in large serving bowls on the table. There were baked beans, salad, steak fries, and baskets of fresh bread.

Gemma looked at Tobias. "This is wonderful."

"And it tastes as good as it looks."

She smiled at Hester. "I'm Gemma. Cassidy's maid of honor."

"Oh, hi. I'm Hester. I'm just the sister of Tanner's girlfriend."

"Nice to meet you."

Tobias nudged Hester. "You're not just anything. You're the dinner companion of the best man."

She blushed again. "I guess I am."

Deacon and Cassidy were seated at another table. When he stood and whistled, everyone turned to look at him.

"I know this is the wrong dinner to be making a toast, but..." He lifted his bottle of beer. "I'd like to thank you all for coming to help us celebrate our upcoming wedding. I know most of you never thought this day would come. Me, getting married. But it did. In a few days, I'll be marrying this beautiful woman." He winked at Cassidy. "For some reason, she agreed to it. Anyway. A toast to friends and family, borrowed from our Scottish ancestors. My great-grandfather was born in Scotland and somehow ended up on the Texas panhandle. To you, grandpa, and to all of you."

"May there always be work for your hands to do. May your purse always hold a coin or two. May the sun always shine upon your window pane. May a rainbow be certain to follow each rain. May the hand of a friend always be near to you and May God fill your heart with gladness to cheer you."

The toast was met with cheering, and Tobias stood and whistled. Gemma smiled at him as he sat down. "Do you suppose your great-grandfather always wanted to be a cowboy?"

"Doesn't every kid at some point in his life want to be a cowboy?"

Preston frowned. "I didn't."

Tobias looked at him. "What did you want to be when you were a kid?"

"President."

Tobias looked at Gemma and gave her a wink. "Okay. I hope you get there, Preston."

Riley, who had just tuned into the conversation, laughed. "President Preston. That's funny."

Tobias smiled. "And what do you want to be when you grow up, Riley?"

"I don't know. I think a fireman. Or a football player."

Tobias gave him a thumbs up. "Good goals."

Riley laughed. "What did you want to be when you were a kid?"

"A cowboy. Actually, I wanted to be a really good horseman. But that didn't happen. I'm just an average cowboy."

"Do you like it?"

"What's not to like? I get to ride horses all day. Chase cows around once in a while. Fish in the pond on a slow day. It's pretty fun."

"Sounds like it." He looked at Gemma. "Mom. Can I ride a horse?"

She glanced at Tobias. "I don't know, honey."

Tobias pointed at him. "Little man, if you want to ride a horse, and it's okay with your mom. I can arrange that."

"Cool. Can I, Mom? Can I?"

"We'll talk about it."

He looked at Tobias. "That means yes."

Tobias smiled at Gemma. "So, we heard what all us guys wanted to be when we were kids." He turned toward Hester. "How about you?"

"I want to be a veterinarian."

"That's awesome." He looked at Gemma.

She smiled and glanced at Riley. "I wanted to be a doctor like my dad."

Tobias nodded. "Well, you almost made it."

"I did. And I like what I do. If I'd pursued medicine, I'd still be in school."

Riley patted her hand. "Mom helps people feel better."

Tobias looked at Gemma. "So I've heard."

Chapter Seven

"The eternal love optimist."

Abby and Skyler were sitting at the far end of Deacon and Cassidy's table. Abby watched her brother for a moment.

"He's really happy. I never thought it'd happen."

"I guess when the right woman comes along, it changes everything."

Abby nudged him. "Listen to you being all romantic."

Skyler laughed. "I'm just saying."

"Right." She took a bite of steak and looked around at the guests sitting at their table. "I don't see anyone here who'd be a good match for you."

"A good match? Now you sound like my mother."

"Sorry. I didn't mean it that way. Half of these people are my cousins. But not on the Carmichael side. My dad was an only child."

He turned in his seat toward her. "So, they're not worthy of marrying a Fremont?"

"Well. We have to find someone you want to marry. But she also has to appeal to your folks."

"Yeah. I don't see that happening. You're probably the only woman here who'd they approve of. Although there is the whole Carmichael rivalry."

"Which is only in your father's head." She patted his hand. "But you're sweet."

He studied her for a moment. "Hmm. Yeah. I am, aren't I?" He turned back to the table. "So did you find yourself a city boy to date at college?"

She laughed. "No. They're all so... I don't know. I thought that'd be the one interesting thing about going to school away from here. That I'd meet someone who wasn't one of the Texas Ten. Or wishes their family was one of the Texas Ten."

"No luck?"

"No. They're stupid. And boring. All they talk about is video games or superhero movies. 'Have you seen so and so in concert?' I don't even know who so and so is."

He laughed. "You've been sheltered here on the Starlight Ranch. And in Connelly."

"Maybe. But if I have, then I'm fine with it. Thank you, Deacon."

"He did alright."

She nudged him. "Just alright?"

"He did fantastic. You're a star, Abby. One in a million."

"Well now you're going to make me blush."

———————⊱✦⊰———————

Gemma sought out Cassidy after dinner. She hadn't seen much of her during the day and she wanted to spend a little time with her friend. About half of the guests had gone home, and she found Cassidy sitting on a bench in front of one of the portable firepits set on the grass. With the sun going down, it was cooling off.

"There you are." She had two glasses of wine and she handed one to Cassidy.

She took the wine as Gemma sat next to her.

"I'll tell you what, your cowboys know how to throw a barbecue."

"Wasn't it great?"

"It was amazing. And I don't think I've ever had a better steak."

"Carmichael beef. You can't beat it."

Gemma looked at her for a moment. "You seem very happy."

"I am. Deacon is... Well, you've been around him."

"Yes, I have. He's quite..."

"Perfect?"

"Yeah. That works." They touched glasses. "I'm sorry your grandpa didn't make it."

"I just hope he gets out of the hospital before the wedding."

"Do you think he will?"

Cassidy shrugged. "I don't know. He's pretty sick, still."

"Riley and I will pray for him tonight."

"Thank you.

"I bet he's happy you're marrying a local rancher. And a Carmichael, to boot."

"He is. He and Deacon have already been strategizing how best to combine the two ranches when he retires and turns it over to me. Which will be sooner than later if his health continues to decline."

"And what about your folks? Are they coming for the wedding?"

"I don't think so. Dad refuses to return to his roots. And Mom won't come without him."

"I'm sorry."

Cassidy shook her head. "It's fine. I don't need any family drama at my wedding. And if they came, there would be problems."

"You've got a wonderful family right here on this ranch. And a lot of people from town were here. So they must like you, too."

She laughed. "Half of them were related to the Carmichaels. The other half just wanted a good steak."

Gemma drank some wine. "I sat across the table from Tobias at dinner."

Cassidy turned toward her. "How'd that go?"

Gemma shrugged. "He's pretty sweet when he's not mad at me."

"He is very sweet. And quite funny. Though you probably haven't seen that side of him."

"I saw a glimpse of it in Malady Springs."

"I really wish you didn't live so far away. I'd love to have you closer. And I'd love for you and Tobias to make a go of it."

Gemma sighed. "I wouldn't mind that either. He's really, really sexy."

Cassidy laughed. "Yeah. These Carmichael boys have it going on."

They were both laughing when Deacon came up behind Cassidy and kissed her on the neck.

"What am I interrupting here?"

"Girl talk."

"Hmm. You're talking about me, right?"

"We were talking about the Carmichael men in general."

He knelt next to her chair. "About how charming we are?"

"Yep."

"And irresistible?"

"That, too."

Gemma leaned forward in her chair and held her hands over the flames. "And modest."

Deacon laughed. "And a bit full of shit."

Cassidy kissed him. "That's okay. You have just the right amount of it. I wouldn't want you to be too perfect."

He stood. "Speaking of being full of shit, have you seen my brother?"

"Tobias?"

"Of course. Tanner is still sweet and mostly innocent. Which is surprising, considering both Hallie and Hester Wexler are in love with him."

Gemma looked at him. "Both of them? Tobias escorted Hester to dinner. She seems sweet."

"Yeah. Her feelings are unrequited. Currently, Tanner is dating Hallie. But Hester has had her eye on him for a while."

"Oh my goodness."

"Yeah. Poor girl. I'm actually rooting for Hester. She seems like a much better match for Tanner. But right now, he only has eyes for the cheerleader."

Cassidy patted Deacon's hand. "It will all work itself out."

Deacon bent and kissed her on the top of her head. "The eternal love optimist." He looked at Gemma. "She believes true love will conquer all."

Gemma smiled. "That's lovely. I hope she's right."

"Okay. I'm going to go track down Tobias. He was moving a little slow last I saw him. He might be in for a bad night."

"Which means, what?"

"Which means he'll be self-medicating with rum."

Cassidy watched Deacon go, then looked at Gemma. "Can anything be done for Tobias? Or is he destined to live in pain the rest of his life? It seems like a harsh sentence for a twenty-seven-year-old."

"Not knowing anything about his injury, I can't say for sure. But surely some of the stuff I do with my athletes would help. Of course, he'd need to be willing to accept help, and it seems he's dead set against it at this point."

"He's been through a lot. Seen all the doctors. Deacon is a bulldog when it comes to things like that. Never give up. Tobias finally had to say enough. He was done with it all."

"Do you know what happened?"

"He was a world-class jumper on his way to trying out for the Olympics."

"Seriously?"

"Yeah. Apparently, he was really good. But his horse took a jump wrong, and they both went down. The horse landed on Tobias. And I guess rolled back and forth several times before getting to her feet. Tobias was in a coma for days."

"Oh my gosh."

"Yeah. It was bad. Deacon was sure he'd lost his brother. And this was just six years after they lost their dad when he fell off a horse and hit his head."

"Faith must've been devastated."

"She never knew it was a horse that did it. Deacon told her Tobias was in a car accident. I don't know if you've noticed, but Faith is quite...fragile. She's been pretty present since you've arrived. I think the wedding and all has her distracted. But she never recovered from losing her husband. And she doesn't want to hear about her kids on horses."

"That's horrible."

"That's why my dear Deacon is so preoccupied with taking care of everything and everybody. He's been doing it since he was twenty-three."

"So even the happiest of families have their demons to deal with."

"Yeah. But in this case, they all came out stronger for it. Everyone but Faith, that is."

Deacon still hadn't found Tobias by the time everyone left. So, after checking the barn one more time, he went to the house and knocked on Tobias' bedroom door.

"Tobias, you in there?"

"No."

"I'm coming in."

"Leave me alone, please."

Deacon opened the door and went into the room. Tobias was lying on the bed and lifted his head to frown at Deacon. "Are you getting hard of hearing in your old age?"

"No. But I've perfected selective hearing." He moved to the bed and nodded at the half-empty bottle of rum. "How much was in the bottle when you started?"

"Actually, it was three-fourths full. It's not doing the trick tonight. So, I figured why waste it." He studied Deacon for a moment. "You look like you've had a few."

"It was my party." Deacon looked down at him. "Are you having a bad night?"

"Yeah. One of those nights that makes me wish they'd just cut the bastard off."

Deacon shook his head. "Don't say that. What can I do?"

"Do you have a hacksaw?"

"Stop. What did you do today? Why the flareup?"

Tobias shrugged. "I spent the morning on Aladdin, but nothing too crazy. We took a short trail ride. I didn't jump over any obstacles.

Didn't even go uphill. It might be the ride combined with standing all afternoon and being sociable."

"Being sociable makes your leg hurt?"

"No. But the standing does sometimes."

Deacon took a couple steps back from the bed. "I'm going to go get Gemma."

"Why? No. Screw that."

"Maybe she can help you. When you start asking for a hacksaw, it worries me."

"I was kidding. Mostly."

"Exactly. I'll be back."

He tried to sit up. "Seriously, man. Don't."

Deacon stopped and looked at him. "If you can get up off the bed and stop me, I won't go get her."

Tobias scowled, then flipped Deacon off. "You're a bastard."

"It runs in the family." He left and went downstairs to the guest bedroom, then knocked on the door. After a moment, Gemma opened it.

Deacon smiled. "Hi. Sorry to bother you."

"Is something wrong?"

"Um... It's Tobias. Let me start by saying he was totally against me talking to you."

"Okay. Talking to me about what?"

"He's in pain pretty much all the time. But usually, he handles it and doesn't let it slow him down too much. Sometimes, though, it gets bad. Once in a while it gets really bad. Tonight it's really bad. His go to pain duller isn't even working."

"Rum?"

Deacon nodded. "Yeah. I was hoping you might be able to suggest something to ease his pain a little. It's what you do, right?"

"Yes. It's what I do. Hold on a minute. I'll be right out."

She closed the door and Deacon waited for her to come out. When she did, he gave her a small smile. "I don't mean to put you in an awkward situation. If you want to just talk me through it."

"Take me to him."

"Right. Let's go."

He went back upstairs with Gemma right behind him. When they got to Tobias' room, he tapped, then opened the door.

"I'm back. And Gemma's with me."

They went inside, and Tobias glared at Deacon before nodding to Gemma. "I'm sorry. My brother has never been able to take no for an answer when he thinks he can fix something. He won't accept that this problem can't be fixed."

Gemma went to the bed. "Where does it hurt?"

He looked at her for a moment. "My thigh. On the outside, mostly. From the knee to the hip."

"And what have you done for it?"

"I drank a quarter bottle of rum. To no avail."

"Can I touch you?"

He glanced at Deacon. "Um...sure."

Gemma put her hands on his thigh. "Your muscles are in knots. No wonder it hurts so much."

"Is that what they pay you the big bucks for? To state the obvious?"

Deacon cleared his throat. "Tobias, be nice. She's trying to help."

"Sorry."

Gemma gently rubbed his thigh. "I can massage the area. It'll help a little. Hopefully enough to let you sleep."

"Fine. I guess. It can't get worse."

"Do you have any lotion or oil?"

He looked at her. "Do I look like the kind of guy who has lotion or oil?"

She turned to Deacon, and he headed for the door.

"I'll go get some from Cassidy."

Chapter Eight

"I haven't always made the best choices."

After Deacon left, Gemma looked around the room. "This isn't what I expected. It's like an apartment."

"You thought we were all just living with our mom?"

"I didn't really think about it."

"I'm building a house. It should be ready before next winter sets in. It's on a spot Deacon picked out for himself. He figured he was never going to get married, so he planned on moving into his own place. Of course, Cassidy changed all that. Being the first son, with the first wife, the house is his. Besides, when Mom's bad, Deacon is the only one who can calm her down. He needs to stay here for her."

"You're building it yourself?"

"Well, I've got help. I'm not a carpenter, by any means. But I can pound a nail and man a saw."

Deacon came back through the door with a bottle of lotion in his hand. "This was the least feminine smelling stuff she had."

Gemma smiled. "I'm sure it'll be fine." She held it up to Tobias. "Almond and vanilla."

"My favorite."

Deacon retreated toward the door. "I guess I'll leave you to it."

Gemma turned to him. "Can you help him take his jeans off first?"

Tobias tried to sit up. "I can undress myself." He dropped back down. "Well, maybe I need a little help."

Deacon helped him out of his jeans, then Tobias pulled the blanket over his mid-section.

He looked at Gemma. "I know you've seen me naked, but this is a little awkward."

"Just relax, Tobias."

Deacon headed for the door again. "I'll be in my room if you need anything else."

Gemma smiled at him. "Thank you, Deacon." She turned back to Tobias. "I'm going to start off gentle, and gradually use more pressure. But if it hurts too much, let me know and I'll back off."

"Got it." He shook his head. "I'm sorry, but everything you say sounds sexual to me."

"I'm just a therapist right now." She sat next to him and squeezed some lotion onto his thigh, then started massaging it. "Is that pressure okay?"

He smiled. "Yeah."

"Tobias. Behave." She applied a little too much pressure, and he flinched.

"That'll teach me."

She lighten her touch. "Did they repair the bone, or did they replace it?"

"It's held together with several pins, screws, superglue. I don't know."

She continued massaging his thigh. "Do you have pain in your calf?"

"Not much. It's not noticeable over the pain in my thigh."

She moved higher on his leg. "Does it go into your buttocks or down into your knee?"

"No. Somehow, my knee survived the incident. I'm not sure how." He winced when she hit a sore spot.

"When your muscles are this tense, it exacerbates the pain. Do you ever use ice or heat?"

"Both. Ice seems to do more than heat does."

"Have you iced it today?"

"After dinner for a while. Thirty minutes or so. Then the ice melted, and I didn't want to get up and get more."

"Is this helping?"

"Yeah. I think it is." It felt really good, but he wasn't sure if it was just because it was her touching him. Or if it would feel the same if a stranger was doing it.

"You should hire a masseuse. If you had regular massage, it would help a lot. It'd keep your muscles from cramping up like this."

"How about I hire you? You could fly up every few weeks and...do your thing."

She ignored his suggestion. "You should do this at least once a week. Along with some exercise."

"I'm a working cowboy. I get plenty of exercise."

"I mean, you need to target the specific muscles in your leg. To strengthen them. And stretching will help too. Your muscles have shortened from you not using them."

"I use them plenty. I don't let this slow me down."

"I realize that. But you favor the leg. Even if you don't know you're doing it. Logically, a person believes they'll avoid pain by not doing certain things that might make it hurt. But actually, in the long run, it makes things worse."

"So you think I should do something that hurts and that I know will put me out of commission?"

"Yes. It will make it better over time."

He shook his head. "That makes no sense to me."

"Tobias?"

"Hmm."

"How long have you been in pain?"

"Five plus years."

She stopped massaging for a moment. "So, would it hurt for you to try something new on the off chance that it might help?"

"I guess not." He was quiet for a moment, then he looked at her. "Can I ask you a question?"

"Sure."

"Do you think about our night in Malady Springs?"

"Of course I do." She began rubbing his leg again.

"It was good, right? I'm not remembering it wrong?"

"It was good, Tobias."

He put his hand over hers. "I need you to stop for a moment while I say this. You and I together that night was amazing. And it wasn't because we'd had too much to drink. Or the fact we were playing the damn, no personal information game. It was because that moment was meant to happen. We were destined to run into each other in that bar."

"You don't strike me as someone who believes in destiny."

"I'm not. Or at least I never have been. But when it steps up and slaps you in the face, you kind of have to pay attention."

"So, is it destiny I showed up here two days later?"

"No. That was just God messing with me."

She smiled at him. "You think God messes with people?"

"He and I haven't had the best track record together. I'm not complaining or feeling sorry for myself. I just think when I was sixteen, He pointed a finger at me and said, that one. That's the one I'm going to mess with. First, I'll take his dad from him. Then I'll get his hopes up by letting him get to within two months of the Olympic trials, before dropping a horse on him."

"Are you sure you're not feeling a little sorry for yourself?"

"Maybe I am. But putting you in my path and then snatching you away. That was the cruelest joke of all."

"Tobias."

"You don't need to say anything. I know nothing I say really matters and it won't change things. When the wedding's over, you've got a life to return to. I get that. And I wouldn't want to interfere in any way. It just sucks. That's all."

He removed his hand, and she started massaging his thigh again. "I'm sorry things didn't work out differently. I wish I didn't live in Austin. I really do."

"But you do."

"Yeah. I do. Do you wish it'd never happened?"

"Never. I'll never wish for that. That night was the closest to heaven I'll ever get."

"You don't think you're going to heaven some day?"

"I think it's a crap shoot. I haven't always made the best choices. I drink too much. I've fallen in love a few too many times, but I'm not a womanizer. Though you may disagree with that. But the biggest obstacle might be that I think He singled me out. He may have a problem with that."

She stopped and took his hand. "Tobias. You're a much better person than you think you are."

"How do you figure? You've only known me for two days and one night."

"I've seen how you are with my son. And the way you love your family. I'm pretty sure you'd do anything for them, including dying for them if it came down to it. I also know what happened with Cassidy. You were man enough to step away and let her and Deacon become what they are now."

"Well, I was a little pissed at first. Culminating in me spending a small fortune on a stubborn horse who's barely worth half of what I spent."

"Aladdin?"

"Yeah. Stubborn bastard."

"You're a good man, Tobias."

He sighed. "A good man who's going to spend the rest of his life alone, because every time a good woman comes into his life—"

"You'll get your shot."

"I'll believe it when I see it. Are you sure you don't want to be my personal masseuse? That would solve a lot of problems. For me anyway. And it'd free Preston up to run for president."

Gemma laughed. "Poor Preston. He can't help being pretentious."

"Hmm. I can think of a more fitting adjective."

"Don't. I did date him for a while."

"Yeah. Why? You're so... And he's so..." He shook his head. "Love is blind, I guess."

"I never loved Preston. I thought maybe I did. But now I know I didn't and never could."

"Because you spent the night with a handsome cowboy?"

She laughed. "No. I figured it out long before that. But that night with you, gave me a glimpse of what it's supposed to look like."

He put a hand on his chest. "My heart is breaking right now, Gemma."

"I'm sorry."

"Not as sorry as I am." He sighed. "So what kind of exercises are we talking about to get this leg back in fighting shape?"

"When I get home, I'll do some research and I'll write you up a plan."

"A plan, huh?"

"Yes. You might consider getting someone local to help you with it. A personal trainer. One that works with traumatic injuries. And I'm serious about getting regular massages. At least once a week."

"You've been to Connelly, right? We don't have a plethora of personal trainers and massage therapists. We don't even have a gym. We have a gym teacher, but that guy's not laying hands on me."

Gemma smiled. "I'll see if I can find someone close by. You might have to travel, or have them travel to you. It'll cost you a bit more, but I'm pretty sure you can afford it."

"As long as I stop overpaying for horses."

"You could stop buying rum. Think how much money that'd save you."

"Loads."

She patted his hand, then stood. "Can we be friends now?"

He nodded. "Yes. No more grumpy Tobias."

"Maybe when your leg calms down you can take Riley and me on a trail ride."

He smiled. "Wow. Interesting. Do we have to bring Preston?"

"No. Besides, I don't think you could pay him to get on a horse."

"Have you ridden before?"

"I rode a horse in summer camp eleven years ago."

"So, the answer is no."

"I guess it is."

He sat up a little and leaned against the headboard. "I've got just the horse for you. And Riley can ride with me."

"Sounds good." She got to her feet. "I should get back."

"You don't want to keep Preston waiting."

"I'm sure Preston is sound asleep next to Riley, and doesn't even know I'm gone."

He looked up at her. "I'll see you at breakfast."

"Good night, Tobias."

"Night. And thank you."

Chapter Nine

"So there's no hanky-panky going on?"

When Deacon and Cassidy came down for breakfast, Ruthie was coming from Faith's room. She went to Deacon.

"Your mother's having a bad day."

"Should I go see her?"

"It might be a good idea. I brought her some breakfast, but she said she wasn't hungry."

Deacon squeezed Cassidy's hand. "Go ahead and start breakfast. I'll be there when I can."

"Okay."

He walked to Faith's door, then opened it and went inside.

"Mother?"

"Oh, honey. Please take this tray away. I really don't think I can eat it."

She was sitting on her favorite couch by the window, and the tray was on a table in front of the couch. Deacon sat next to her. There was a deer and two fawns on the grass about a hundred feet from the house.

"My deer family is back."

"She had twins this year."

"Aren't they precious?"

They watched the deer for a few minutes, then Deacon glanced at the tray of food. "Why don't you eat a couple bites of this before it gets cold?"

"I'm not hungry."

"You know how Ruthie gets when you don't eat her food."

Faith smiled. "She hates to see food go to waste. When you were a baby, you went through a stage where you wouldn't eat anything. She'd tried so many things until she found something you'd eat. It was the only time I saw her toss uneaten food. The pigs ate well that summer."

"How old was I?"

"Two or three. You were such a beautiful baby." His mother reminiscing about things that happened a long time ago, was usually a prequel to her disassociating and believing her husband was alive.

"Let's not let this food go to the pigs. Just a few bites."

Faith turned towards the tray. "Very well." She picked up the fork. "Will you stay with me while I eat?"

"Of course."

She took a bite. "I believe the Fremont boy has his eye on your sister."

"I think they're just friends."

"No. It's more than that. Keep an eye on him."

"Wouldn't that be a good thing? A Carmichael marrying a Fremont?"

"Oh, the boys okay. But the family is a mess. I wouldn't want Abby to have to deal with crazy in-laws."

"I'm sure Abby could hold her own."

"Of Course. But she shouldn't have to. I was lucky your grandparents were so welcoming to me. Your father was a catch. And he could've married someone a lot better than me."

"Mother."

"From a better family. We had even less money than Winston O'Hare."

"Mother. I don't care how much money Cassidy's family has. The whole money thing is outdated. It's more about politics than money these days. And I don't buy into it."

"I know you don't. You're a good man. Like your father. He married for love. As you are doing. I'm very proud of you."

"Thank you, Mother."

She took some more bites and Deacon could see her fading away. She was starting to slip.

He patted her arm. "Are you okay, Mother?"

"Of course." She set her fork down. "I think I'll save the rest of this until your father gets back."

"Okay. Do you want me to take it to the kitchen?"

"No. He'll be back soon. Go check on your brothers and sister. You know how much mischief they can get into when you don't keep an eye on them."

Deacon got to his feet. "I'll make sure they stay out of trouble."

"Thank you, honey."

———————————⁂———————————

The rest of the family, along with Gemma, Preston, and Riley, were at the table when Deacon came into the dining room. He gave Cassidy a small smile when he sat next to her.

"Is everything okay?"

He shook his head.

Tobias caught on to what was going on and reached for a piece of ham. He dropped it onto Deacon's plate. "Eat up, brother."

"Thanks."

"So, what's the plan today?"

When Deacon didn't answer, Cassidy spoke up. "Today, we're taking a breather. We're going to enjoy the fact Abby is home. And take it easy."

Tobias grinned at her. "You're going to take it easy, four days before your wedding?"

"I'm going to try to take it easy."

Gemma took a sip of orange juice. "And tomorrow is my and Abby's dress fitting, right?"

"Yes. We want to make sure they fit you perfectly."

Tobias nodded. "That's good. Because we guys don't want to outshine you. I'm not bragging, but we look damn good in our wedding outfits."

Gemma smiled. "I'm sure you do."

Deacon pulled himself out of his depressed mood. "But tomorrow morning is the family trail ride. Just the four of us." He looked at Tobias. "Are you up for it? We can postpone."

"No. I'm good."

On most holidays, all birthdays, and now weddings, the Carmichael siblings rode to the twisted oak tree at the far end of the valley. Ten and a half years ago, they spread their father's ashes under it. They'd go there to pay their respects and each of them would take a few moments alone to fill their father in on what had been going on in their lives. Faith hadn't returned to the tree since the day they spread the ashes. She also hadn't been on a horse since that day. The day she buried her husband, she also buried the horsewoman who'd once been a rodeo queen and won the heart of a bronc riding cowboy.

After breakfast, Gemma followed Tobias onto the porch. "How's the leg?"

He patted his leg. "It's good. Thanks to you."

"Are you just saying that?"

"No. It's feels fine. In fact, if you're still down to take that trail ride. I'm game."

She studied him for a moment. "Are you sure? I don't want you to be sore for your family ride tomorrow."

"The ride with you is going to be laid back. No different than if I was sitting here on the porch."

"It's a little different."

He smiled at her. "Do you want to go, or not?"

"Yes, please. Riley will be extremely excited."

"And what's Preston going to do?"

She shrugged. "Don't know. And really don't care. He can entertain himself."

Tobias' smile turned into a grin. "Are you getting a little perturbed with Preston?"

She sighed. "I can't help but compare him to you and your brothers."

"You mean real men?"

"Wow. Let's not go that far. Let's say men who are down to earth and appreciate life and nature. Men who love their family and the lives they're leading."

Tobias held up a hand. "Stop, you're going to make my head swell."

"When are we taking our ride?"

"How about in an hour? I'll have Ruthie pack us a lunch."

"I get the feeling Ruthie is the glue holding this family together."

"She is." He leaned in close and lowered his voiced. "But don't tell Deacon. He thinks it's him."

She put a finger to her lips. "It'll be our secret."

Abby came through the door and smiled at them. "Am I interrupting?"

Gemma returned her smile. "No." She pointed at Tobias. "I'll see you later."

Abby watched her go inside, then slapped Tobias on the chest. "What's going on with you two?"

"Nothing. I'm taking her and Riley on a little trail ride."

"Fun. Has she ridden before?"

"Nope. I thought I'd put her on old Raven."

She nodded. "That should work. He's what? A hundred years old?"

"Not quite. He just moves like he's a hundred years old."

Abby nudged him. "So are you guys friends now?"

"We came to an agreement last night. Mostly, I agreed not to be grumpy anymore."

"Okay. Happy Tobias is so much more fun than grumpy Tobias. And speaking of grumpy Tobias. Is Aladdin ready for me to ride?"

"Wow. Um...yes. I think."

"Should I work with him in the pen for a while?"

Tobias nodded. "That'd probably be a good idea."

"Okay, I know how I'm spending my morning."

"Sorry. I tried to have him ready."

"It's fine. I should've asked Tanner to work with him."

"Hey." Abby cocked her head, and Tobias nodded. "Okay. You're right. Tanner is better in the training pen."

She smiled. "I'm going to tell him you said so."

"No. Don't. It'll go right to his head."

"No, it won't. Tanner is sweet. He'll just be flattered you think so highly of him."

"Don't tell him that, either."

Abby headed for the barn, and Tobias went into the house to track down Ruthie. He found her in the kitchen, where she spent most of her time.

"Good morning, Ruthie. That was an excellent breakfast this morning."

She looked up from the dough she was kneading. "What do you want?"

He put a hand to his chest. "Can't a man come in here and compliment you without an ulterior motive?"

"A man can. You never do."

He grinned. "You know I love you, Ruthie."

"Yes, I know. Now tell me what you want. I've got bread to knead."

"I was hoping you could find time in your busy bread-making schedule, and in your heart, to make me a picnic lunch."

She eyed him suspiciously. "Since when do you go on picnics?"

"I go on picnics." He thought for a moment. "Maybe not in a while."

"Who's going on this picnic?"

"Me, Gemma, and Riley."

Ruthie cocked her head at him and put a towel over the dough, then went to the sink and washed her hands. As she was drying them, she looked at him.

"What are you up to?"

"I'm not up to anything. Gemma asked me to take her and Riley on a ride." He opened the refrigerator door. "But if you're too busy, I'll make it myself."

Ruthie took his arm and pulled him away, then closed the refrigerator door. "Get out of my kitchen. I'll have your picnic ready in thirty minutes."

Tobias smiled. "Thanks, Ruthie." As he left, he ran into Deacon, coming in. He lowered his voice. "Watch out for her. She's in a mood."

Ruthie called out, "I heard that."

Deacon came into the kitchen and poured himself a cup of coffee. "What's that all about?"

Ruthie returned to her dough. "You tell me. Seems your brother is taking Miss Gemma and her son on a trail ride."

Deacon smiled. "Oh, good."

"How is that good? You know Tobias has a tendency to fall for unavailable women."

"In this case, it's okay. And they're just friends."

"And the boyfriend?"

"He's a non-issue."

She raised an eyebrow. "Does he know that?"

Deacon laughed. "Yes. I believe he does."

"So there's no hanky-panky going on?"

"No, Ruthie. No hanky-panky."

Chapter Ten

"Do I get a cowboy hat, too?"

Tobias was in the barn saddling Raven when Preston came up behind him.

"Excuse me."

Tobias glanced over his shoulder and was surprised to see who it was. "What can I do for you, Preston?"

"Gemma said you were taking her and Riley out horseback riding."

"That's right." He tightened the cinch, before turning to Preston. "Do you have a problem with that?"

"No. I want to make sure you know they've never ridden before."

"I'm aware."

"So...you'll be careful?"

"Of course." He put his hand on Raven. "This horse, which Gemma will be riding, is so slow, he damn near walks backwards. Gemma will be fine."

"And Riley?"

"Riley will be riding with me on my horse, Chance, who is very well trained and has gotten me through more than one tight situation. I trust Chance with my life."

"Okay." Preston nodded. "I'm just making sure."

Tobias hated the question he was about to say, and he hoped Gemma meant what she said about Preston and horses. "You're welcome to come with us."

Preston took a step back. "No. Thank you. I trust you'll keep them safe."

"You don't need to worry about them. They'll be fine."

"Okay. Um... I'll leave you to it."

Tobias watched Preston until he left the barn, then turned to Raven. "Interesting. I'll give him a few props for that."

When Gemma and Riley came into the barn, she approached Tobias and handed him the picnic tote. "I just ran into Preston leaving the barn. What did he want?"

"He wanted to make sure I wasn't putting you on a wild and crazy horse."

"I'm sorry."

"No. It's fine. I understand where he's coming from. I guess." He attached the tote to the back of Raven's saddle, then looked at Riley. "Hmm. Something is missing."

Riley looked down at his jeans and t-shirt. "I don't think so."

"I'll be right back." Tobias went to a storage area and returned a few minutes later with a child-sized cowboy hat. "I think this should fit."

Riley jumped up and down. "For me? I can wear it? Is it a real cowboy hat?"

"Yes, it is." He put the hat on Riley. "This is an official Carmichael cowboy hat. I believe Tanner and Abby both wore it when they were your age."

"Cool."

"Are you ready to ride?"

Riley nodded.

"Okay. Let me get your mother up on Raven, then we'll put you on Chance." He looked at Gemma. "Are you ready?"

"Do I get a cowboy hat, too?"

"If you want one."

"I think I'm okay for today." She looked at the horse. "Okay. How do I do this?"

Tobias took her arm and led her around to the left side of the horse. "Put your left leg into the stirrup, then put your weight on it and throw your right leg over the saddle. Easy as pie."

"Hmm. We'll see." She did as he told her and found herself in the saddle. "Oh, my goodness. I did it."

Tobias handed her the reins. "Don't do anything. Just sit there until I get on Chance."

She gave him a nervous smile. "Don't worry. I'm not moving a muscle."

Tobias picked up Riley. "Okay. Up you go." Riley settled into the saddle with a grin. "Hold on to the saddle horn and don't move around too much." Tobias got into the saddle behind Riley. "Good job." He looked at Gemma. "That was the hard part. Are you ready to move now?"

"Hold on." She took her cell phone from her back pocket. "Let me get a picture of you two."

"How about I get down and you get a picture of the little man?"

"I'd like you in the picture, Tobias. Do you mind?"

"Not at all." He and Riley both smiled while Gemma took several pictures. "Okay. Okay. That's enough." When Gemma started to stash her phone in her back pocket, he pointed at her. "You might want to put that in your jacket pocket. Phones tend to wiggle out when you're on the back of a horse."

She put it into the pocket of her jacket. "I guessing you know this from firsthand experience."

"I've got at least a couple of phones lying out there somewhere in the tall grass."

Gemma laughed. "You think you'd learn from the first one."

"You'd think. I guess I'm not too smart sometimes." He put a hand on Riley, before taking the reins in his other hand. "Let's hit the trail."

"What do I do?"

"Hang on to the reins. Raven will follow Chance."

Tobias clicked his tongue, and Chance started moving. Raven moved as soon as he realized Chance was, and Gemma let out a squeal.

"You're fine. Relax and move with the horse. If you try to fight it, you'll be sore tomorrow."

They left the barn and headed for the pasture. After going through a gate, they were in knee-high grass. After a few minutes, Gemma seemed to be confident enough to look around.

"It's so beautiful out here."

Tobias looked at her. "Yeah. It is." He stopped the horses. "Hand me your phone." Gemma took it from her pocket and held it out to him. "Alright. We need a picture of you on the back of a horse. You can go back home and show all your coworkers what a cowgirl you are." He held up the phone. "Smile."

Gemma smiled while Tobias took two pictures. "Okay. Let me see them."

Tobias went to her gallery and checked them out. "Perfect."

"Let me have my phone back."

"Hold on." He held the phone in front of Riley. "Ready for a selfie?"

Riley giggled and Tobias took a few pictures in which they were both making faces. He handed the phone to Gemma. "Put it away now. This is a trail ride, not a photo shoot."

She looked at the pictures, then returned the camera to her pocket. "You two are a couple of really silly boys."

"Okay. No more fun. Horseback riding is serious business."

Riley looked at him. "No it's not. It's fun."

"You're right, kid. It is fun." He got the horses moving again. "We're going to go through those trees up there and come out below the ridge I'm building my house on."

Gemma seemed more comfortable in the saddle now. "Oh, cool. I'd love to see it."

They continued to take it slowly, as they crossed the meadow, then wandered through the stand of scrub pine and small oaks. They left the trees and came out onto another meadow that was several acres across. At one end of it was a bluff with his framed house sitting on the edge of it. The other three sides of the meadow ended in more trees.

"What a beautiful view you're going to have."

"We have a herd of wild horses on the property and they favor this valley during the summer and the fall, because the grass stays green. There are several underground springs that pop up here and there. You can see where they're at by the cattails."

Gemma looked over the field. "Oh my goodness. That's amazing. I didn't know there were still wild horses running around."

"This herd has about twenty mares and the stallion. Every year there's a few new babies."

"I'd love to see them."

"It's a little early yet. But they're probably close by keeping an eye on us. We're going to skirt the tall grass, so we don't find ourselves in a bog. Then we'll leave the horses and walk up to the house."

They made their way around the grass, and Tobias stopped Chance at the bottom of the bluff. It was only about twenty feet above the pasture. Just high enough to allow for a perfect view.

Tobias dismounted, then lifted Riley down. He tied Chance to a tree, then went to help Gemma.

"Reverse what you did to get up. Put all your weight on your left foot."

She got down without incident, then smiled at Tobias. "Thank you."

"For what?"

"For putting up with us greenhorns. I'm having an amazing time."

"I'm glad. I love sharing all this with someone who's never seen it. It reminds me to look at it through the eyes of someone who's seeing it for the first time. Makes me appreciate it more."

She put a hand on his arm and gave him a look that made him realize she wanted to be with him as much as he wanted to be with her. She held his gaze for a moment, then looked away and glanced at Riley. "What do you think about all this?"

"It's great!"

Tobias laughed. "It is pretty great. Isn't it?" He tied Raven near Chance. "Okay. Follow me. There's a trail over here that's not too steep." He led them to the trail, and they started walking toward the house.

Gemma glanced at him. "So I'm assuming you have access that doesn't involve riding a horse?"

"There's a rough dirt road that I need to work on. As it is, I'd be stuck here in the winter when it rains and snows. It takes you out to the highway, though, in about five miles."

"Goodness. So you'll be pretty remote."

"I'm going to put in a small shed for Chance. By horse, if you're not a novice, it's thirty minutes to the main house. Not a bad commute to work."

"Sounds perfect."

"Yeah. I think I might get a little lonely, though. At the house, there's always someone around. And of course, I'm going to miss Ruthie's cooking."

"I'm sure you'll do fine. Besides. Your room will always be available, right?"

"Until Cassidy turns it into a nursery."

Gemma laughed. "I guess that is a possibility."

"Yeah. If she can talk Deacon into it. He's not completely onboard with the whole fatherhood thing. But then again, a year ago, he was planning on never getting married. So, there's hope for a new generation of Carmichaels."

They reached the top of the ridge and Riley ran ahead and climbed through the two-by-fours.

Gemma called after him. "Be careful, honey."

"I will."

She looked at Tobias. "So, give me the tour."

"Okay. We need to go in the front door." He took her hand and led her around to the front of the house. "So, all this dirt will be gone once the house is finished. The grass will come back after the first spring. And there will be a big front porch." He took her to a door-sized opening in the two-by-fours. "This is the door."

"Okay."

They stepped through it. Plywood had been laid on the floors except where they were still laying wiring or plumbing. "We're now in the living room. My Uncle Clay is going to build a rock fireplace on that wall. Big windows on these two walls."

"They'll let in lots of light." Riley ran by and went out the front door. "Stay close, Riley."

"I will."

"Through here is the kitchen. Pretty good size. I figure I'll eat in here. No need for a dining room."

Gemma looked around and Tobias could see her trying to envision what it was going to look like. In his mind, he could see her and Riley sitting across the table from him eating breakfast on a sunny morning.

She smiled at him. "I can almost see it."

"Yeah. Me too."

"How many bedrooms?"

"Two. The master bedroom and a guest room that will probably never have a guest in it. Although Tanner might drop by once in a while. Until he goes off to Yale."

"He doesn't seem all that excited to be leaving."

"He's not. Deacon is insisting, though. I didn't want to go either. And Abby really didn't want to go."

"Hmm." They went into the master bedroom.

"I know. Like I said last night. Deacon can be a bulldog when he sets his mind on something. Tanner would rather go to veterinary school somewhere close by. He's got a real way with animals."

"Maybe Deacon will change his mind."

"Maybe. But not likely. Somehow, he feels a business degree is more helpful. We live on a ranch. My business degree has been useless."

Gemma smiled. "I can't quite picture you in business school."

"You and me both. It wasn't a good look."

Riley ran by again, and Tobias grabbed him and picked him up. "Where are you off to?"

"This is like a giant fort."

Tobias set him down. "Go for it, buddy." They returned to the living room and Tobias moved to the far wall of the living room. "This will open to the back deck. This is where I'll drink my coffee in the morning and watch the sun go down in the evening."

She took in the view. "I love it."

The deck wasn't yet covered, so he slid a piece of plywood to the edge of it. "Have a seat. Might as well let the munchkin run off some energy."

They sat on the edge of the deck and looked out over the grass. From there the springs were more noticeable with the higher grass and cattails.

Gemma glanced at Tobias. "This is great. It's going to be beautiful."

"Thanks."

"Please don't tell me you're going to live here alone, forever."

He took a moment to answer her. "Well, I don't currently have any prospects. But ideally, I'd like to share the place with someone."

She nodded. "Good. You deserve to have someone to share it with."

Tobias was quiet while he considered that the only person he wanted to share it with, was sitting right next to him. He gave her a smile. "So, if I'm not prying too much. Who and where is Riley's dad?"

"I have no idea where he is. He's not in the picture."

"I'm sorry."

"Don't be. He was a mistake. And he has no interest, so that's fine with me. Makes things a lot easier."

"I suppose it does."

"But I guess my guilt over Riley not having a father is why Preston is still around. He's not a great boyfriend. But he and Riley are pretty tight."

"That's good."

She looked at him. "But it's time to cut the cord. Riley can still see Preston, of course. But this trip is kind of the last family-like adventure we're going to have."

"He's a good kid. And you may feel guilty he doesn't have a dad. But it seems he's adjusted just fine."

"Thank you for saying that."

"Well, I'm not an expert or anything. But I know a happy kid when I see one."

Chapter Eleven

"Are you sure you can handle it?"

When Riley came through the opening for the back door and walked across a two-by-four with perfect balance, Gemma picked him up and set him on her lap.

"You're a little monkey, aren't you?"

"No. I'm a cowboy."

Tobias laughed. "You sure are." He slid off the edge of the deck and jumped to the ground below. "How'd you like to check out the creek?"

"Yeah."

Tobias took Riley from Gemma and set him on the ground, before looking at her. "Do you want some help, too?"

She looked at the ground four feet below her. "A little, please."

Tobias put his hands on her waist and lifted her down, then held onto her for a moment. When she looked up at him, he let go and took a step back.

"Right. Let's go look at the creek."

Riley ran ahead. "Where is it?"

"Follow the path down to the grass, then keep going that way, you'll run right into it."

Gemma called out, "Don't go in the water." When Riley didn't respond, she looked at Tobias. "He's going to end up wet, isn't he?"

"That's what being a kid is all about."

They caught up to Riley on the edge of the small creek. It was about ten feet across and the water was so clear you could see the rocky bottom a foot below the surface. The slow current made a pleasant sound as it rippled past them.

"Wow. How pretty."

"About a month ago, the water was a foot higher. It's calmed down now."

Riley was right on the edge of the water. "Mom, can I get my feet wet?"

"I don't know, honey."

Tobias nudged her. "Come on, Mom. We want to get our feet wet."

She smiled at him. "If you go with him."

Tobias sat in the grass and pulled off his boots, then removed his socks. He rolled his jeans up to his knees before standing again. Riley saw him and plopped down to remove his shoes and socks. Then took off his hat. Gemma went to him.

"Why don't we take off your jeans, too?"

Riley didn't hesitate, he stood and removed his jeans. Tobias grinned at Riley's Spiderman underwear.

"Man. I'm jealous. I'm wearing plain old plaid underwear. If I had cool Spiderman briefs, I'd totally take my jeans off, too."

Gemma laughed. "I think I'd pay pretty good money to see that."

Tobias looked at her. "Do you have a twenty?"

"Go wade in the creek."

He took Riley's hand, and they stepped into the water. Tobias looked back at Gemma and mouthed, "Shit!"

"Is it a little cold?"

Riley giggled. "It's super cold."

When they got to the middle of the creek, Tobias looked at Riley. "If you have your balance, I'll let you go. It's kind of slippery."

"I got it."

Tobias let go of his hand, and Riley took one step, then slipped and landed on his bottom in the water. He was shocked at first, then looked at Gemma to see if he was in trouble. When she laughed, he smiled and slapped at the water.

Gemma moved to the edge of the creek. "Oh my gosh, are you okay?"

Tobias looked down at Riley, then took his wallet out of his pocket and smiled at Gemma. "Hold on to this for me." He tossed the wallet to her. "If I don't come out of this, you can have whatever is in there." He sat down in the water next to Riley. "Holy... Jeez, it's cold."

Gemma opened his wallet. "There's a whole lot of cash in here, cowboy."

"I don't like plastic."

"Yet, you have a gold card in here."

"It's for emergencies." He looked at Riley. "What now? Do we just sit here?"

Riley shrugged. "I don't know."

Tobias took off his hat and tossed it to shore. "Hold on to that, too." He grinned at Riley, then laid back in the water and put his head under. He came up a moment later. "Jesus, Mary, and Joseph, that's cold." He brushed his hair back and wiped his face.

Riley looked at Gemma expectantly, and she nodded. "Go ahead. You guys are crazy."

He held onto Tobias' arm and laid back. Tobias pulled him back up right away. Riley coughed, and Tobias asked, "Are you okay?"

Riley nodded, then smiled. "It's really cold. I have a brain freeze."

Tobias got to his feet and picked Riley up. "Okay, kid. Let's get out of here before we freeze to death." He carried him to the sun, then set him down. "It's no fun having a brain freeze if you didn't have ice cream to get there."

Gemma joined them. "Let's get your shirt off, crazy boy." She helped Riley out of this t-shirt, then looked at Tobias. "You too."

He smiled at her. "Are you sure you can handle it?"

"Leave it on, take it off. I don't care either way."

"Hmm. I think you might care a little bit." He unbuttoned his shirt, then took it off and handed it to her.

She smiled. "Nothing I haven't already seen. I work with college athletes."

"Yeah. But this is cowboy muscle."

She looked at him. "I suppose it's a little different. More natural."

"Damn right."

She took the shirts to a tree and hung them to dry, while Tobias and Riley sat down in the grass. They had their backs to her, and she watched them for a moment, then took her phone out and took a couple of pictures. She was having a really hard time not falling in love with Tobias Carmichael.

"Are you guys ready to eat?"

Tobias held up his hand and gave her a thumbs up. Riley looked at him, then did the same. She retrieved the lunch tote from the back of Raven before joining Tobias and Riley.

"Okay, let's see what Ruthie packed for us."

Tobias watched her take three sandwiches from the tote. There were also three small bags of chips, three apples, and three bottles of lemonade. He picked up a sandwich.

"Peanut butter and jelly." He handed it to Riley. "This must be yours."

The other two sandwiches were turkey, Swiss cheese, lettuce, and tomato. He took one and a bag of chips.

"It's been a while since I've been on a picnic. Cassidy and I went on one last fall. It was a day or so before she broke up with me."

"Oh no."

"It's okay. Everything worked out the way it's supposed to." He took a bite of his sandwich. "I wouldn't be here with you and this little cowboy if she hadn't come to her senses."

"Well, then, thank you Cassidy."

He smiled. "Damn right." He looked at Riley. "Sorry, kid."

Riley giggled. "That's okay. It's not the really bad word."

"I don't generally use that one."

"Good. Cause it's really bad."

Tobias looked at Gemma and winked. "How's your sandwich?"

"It's perfect. This day just keeps getting better."

He set his sandwich down. "There is one thing that'd make it better for me." He whispered in Riley's ear, and the boy started laughing. Tobias got to his feet and Gemma looked up at him.

"What are you doing?"

"Put your sandwich down."

"Why?"

He took the sandwich from her hand and set it down, then bent and picked her up.

"Tobias, I swear. If you're doing what I think you're doing. I'll never talk to you again."

He headed for the creek. "It's only fair that you get wet, too."

She glared at him. "Don't you dare."

"It's just water."

"Very, very cold water." She kicked her feet. "I'm serious. Put me down."

Tobias looked at Riley, who was following them. "Uh oh, she's serious."

Riley giggled. "It's just water, Mom."

Tobias reached the creek and waded in a few feet, then looked at Gemma. He shook his head. "I can't do it. I don't want you to never talk to me again." He turned and took her back to shore, then set her down.

She punched his arm. "Oh, my God. You were almost in some serious trouble."

Tobias laughed. "You're really beautiful when you're mad."

"Shut up. Being charming isn't going to help you in this situation."

"Hey. I didn't do anything but carry you to the creek."

"Still." She went back to the food and sat down. Tobias smiled as he sat next to her, and she nudged him. "Stop. You're such a child."

He picked up his sandwich and wiggled his toes that were bright pink from the cold water. "I was just starting to get warm."

"Serves you right."

Riley finished his sandwich and stood. "Can I go play?"

"Yes. Just stay where I can see you."

Tobias picked up two of the apples. "Do you want to give these to the horses?"

Riley nodded and took the apples.

"Just hold them flat in your hand, and they'll take it from you."

"Cool!"

He ran off, and Gemma looked at Tobias. "What am I going to do with you?"

"I have a few ideas."

She shook her head. "How am I supposed to leave after the wedding? You're making it very hard."

"You could stay a while longer."

She cocked her head. "Unfortunately, I need to be an adult and do what grown-up people do."

"And what's that?"

"Go back to work."

He looked at her for a moment. "You've seen my wallet, right? Stay here with me and you don't ever have to work again."

"Tobias. It's so much more complicated than that."

"Only if you let it be."

"I can't talk about this."

"Okay. I understand. I'm asking you to give up everything and that's not fair. I'm sorry. I just... Damn, I really like you, Gemma Stone." He thought for a moment. "Oh, my God. I just got your name."

She laughed. "My parents think they're hilarious."

"I love it. They knew they had something rare."

"Stop. You need to stop."

"Alright. Should I carry you back to the creek? Toss you in? Then you can be mad at me again."

"No. Just stop being so sweet."

"You want me to be grumpy Tobias again?"

She smiled. "No. Find a happy medium. Normal, friendly, kind of funny, not grumpy, and not sexy."

"I'll try. But when you got it. You got it. It's kind of hard to tone down the sexy when—"

"Tobias!"

"Right. Normal. I'll try."

"And it'll help a lot if you put your shirt back on."

He grinned. "I knew you couldn't handle it."

Chapter Twelve

"What's this bull you're spreading around?"

When they finished eating, Tobias, Gemma, and Riley headed back to the ranch. He stopped the horses outside of the barn and lifted Riley to the ground, then held Raven while Gemma got down.

She smiled at him. "Thank you. That was wonderful."

"Anytime."

"And thank you for not dropping me into the creek."

He pointed at her. "That, I'm kind of sorry about."

"You should be."

He shook his head. "Not for almost doing it. I'm sorry I didn't."

She put her hands on her hips. "You're lucky you didn't do it."

Tobias spotted Preston headed their way, and he took a step back. "Here comes our future president."

"Shush." She turned and smiled at Preston.

He nodded at her. "I see everyone made it back in one piece."

"It was great."

Riley ran up to Preston and hugged his legs. "It was the best day ever."

"I'm glad you enjoyed it." He glanced at Tobias. "Thanks for taking them."

"My pleasure."

Preston looked at Gemma. "Want to go rest for a bit before dinner?"

"Sure." She touched Tobias' arm. "Thanks, again."

"You bet."

He watched them go toward the house for a moment, then led the horses into the barn. When he went inside, he found Deacon cleaning out a stall. He tied the horses to a rail and walked over to him.

"What's up?"

"Nothing. Why?"

"You're cleaning a stall. Your go to stress reliever."

Deacon stopped and leaned on the rake. "It's Mother."

"What's wrong?"

"She's still in Never Never land. It's been all day."

"She usually snaps out of it after a few hours."

He started raking again. "And now you know why I'm cleaning a stall."

"What can we do?"

Deacon shrugged. "I don't know. She's in her room waiting for Dad to come home."

"Shit."

He stopped again. "I finally realized why she stares out at the meadow. Before we built the new barn, that was the way Dad came home from the pasture."

"Dammit."

"I know." Deacon leaned the rake against the wall and left the stall. "I'm sorry to drag you down. How was the ride?"

Tobias smiled. "It was...pretty damn perfect."

Deacon patted his shoulder. "So, what are you going to do about this woman?"

"I have no idea. How can I ask her to stay? That wouldn't be right. And I'm sure as hell am not going to move to Austin." He looked at Deacon. "What the hell am I supposed to do?"

Deacon hesitated before answering. "I guess you can hope you're so damn irresistible she can't help but stay."

"Yeah. I'm working on that. Not sure if it's doing the trick."

Deacon grinned. "Keep it up. She's bound to cave. No woman can resist the Carmichael charm."

Abby approached them. "Wow, did I just interrupt a secret brotherhood meeting?"

Tobias looked at her. "Yeah. No girls allowed."

She moved closer. "What's this bull you're spreading around?"

Tobias nudged Deacon. "My older brother was giving me some advice."

Abby eyed Deacon for a moment. "He managed to corral himself a great one. But he doesn't have vast experience with women. So..."

Deacon frowned at her. "Hey."

"Before Cassidy, you didn't date anyone for ten years."

"I dated." When both Abby and Tobias cocked their heads, he added. "A little."

Abby hugged him. "I'll admit, you generally give good advice. As long as it doesn't have anything to do with me. What are we advising on?"

"Tobias and Gemma."

"Ah." She smiled at Tobias. "How was the trail ride?"

"Fantastic." He went to the horses and started unsaddling Chance.

She hugged him. "I'm so happy." She stepped back and looked at him. "But you're not."

"I am. It just in a few days, she'll be gone." He moved away from her and released the cinch, then lifted the saddle off.

"Maybe not for good. You never know."

"I kind of do." He handed the saddle to Deacon, then removed Chance's bridle.

"If it's meant to be. It'll work itself out."

"Everyone keeps saying that to me. But that's putting a lot of faith in fate or destiny. Or serendipity. One of those things." Deacon returned from putting the saddle away, and Tobias handed him the bridle.

"You need to believe." She studied him for a moment as she patted Chance's rump. "How come you're wet?"

Tobias felt his jeans. "Riley and I went into the creek."

"You went swimming?"

"Not exactly."

She led Chance into a stall, while Tobias moved to Raven and loosened the cinch. "So, about Riley. Does the fact that Gemma has a son worry you at all? Is that an issue?"

"No. Not even a little. He's a great kid."

"Right. But you could end up raising him if things go well."

He looked at her, as he pulled Raven's saddle off. "I wouldn't have a problem with that."

"Hmm." She looked at Deacon. "Seems our brother is becoming a responsible adult."

Deacon shook his head. "Never thought it'd happen." He took the saddle from Tobias.

Tobias looked at him. "Unlike you, I don't have an issue with having kids."

"I don't have a problem with it." Deacon set the saddle down on a rack and leaned against it.

Tobias leaned on Raven. "I've never once heard you say, 'when I'm a dad...'"

"That doesn't mean I haven't thought about it."

Abby folded her arms across her chest. "I'm sure Cassidy wants kids. You're going to have kids, right? I was hoping to be an aunt soon."

"Soon? Don't count on soon." He straightened up. "Someday. Plan on someday."

"Deacon?"

He sighed. "I have some reservations, but I'm working on it."

Tobias patted him on the back. "Give the man a break. He's getting married in a few days. That's a big enough step for now."

"Thanks, Tobias."

"Sure. And later, when Abby's gone, you can tell me the real reason you're stalling."

Abby shook her head. "This place is such a boy's club."

Tobias laughed. "We include you plenty."

"I seriously doubt that."

Deacon and Tobias hugged her between them and she squealed. "Stop."

Tobias kissed her on the cheek. "We love our little sister."

She broke away from them and wiped her cheek where he kissed her. "Gross."

"My kisses are gross?"

"Well, I'm sure Gemma doesn't think so. But to me, yes."

Deacon headed for the door. "Okay. Enough of this family time. I'm going to go spend time with my soon to be wife."

Abby called after him. "And the mother of your children?"

Deacon kept walking and flipped her off over his shoulder.

Deacon found Cassidy in their room, going over the seating arrangement for the reception dinner. He came up behind her and kissed her.

"Hey my handsome cowboy. How's your mother?"

"I don't want to talk about her." He knelt beside her. "What are you doing?"

She frowned at the chart in front of her. "Trying to get the seating chart right."

"Why does it matter? You've been stressing over it for weeks."

"I know. I just want everything to be perfect."

"Hey." She looked at him. "This is our day. Yours and mine. It really doesn't matter if you sit Aunt Emma next to Fiona Woodward. Or..."

"Wait, why can't they sit together?"

"They haven't spoken in twenty years."

"Why not?"

"Because Emma stole Fiona's boyfriend."

"Your Uncle Henry?"

"No. Before Henry."

She grumbled and moved some stickers around her seating chart. Deacon stood and took her hand. She looked up at him.

"Come on. Leave it for now."

She sighed and let him pull her to her feet, then she put her arms around his neck. "I'm sorry."

"Tomorrow, give the chart to Ruthie. She knows who everyone is and all the drama."

"You think she'll help me?"

"Yes." He led her to the bed. "Sit. I want to talk to you about something."

"Is something wrong?" She sat down, and Deacon sat next to her.

"No. Nothing is wrong. We're getting married in a couple of days. What could possibly be wrong?"

She laid her head on his shoulder. "How come I'm the one stressing over everything and you're the one who's like, eh, whatever?"

"Are you going to let me tell you what I want to tell you?"

She took a breath. "Yes. I'm sorry."

He took her hand. "I know I've been a little uncommunicative about the whole having children thing."

"More than a little. But that's okay."

"No, it's not and I want to tell you why."

"Okay."

"When my dad died and Mother checked out, it made a lasting impression on me."

"Well, of course it did."

"But not how you think. It left me determined to not do two things. Get married. And have kids."

She gave him a small smile. "Are you breaking up with me?"

He laughed. "God no." He kissed her. "I saw what losing my dad did to the family. How it destroyed my mother. How it left Tobias, Abby, and Tanner without a father."

"You lost your father, too."

"Right, I know. But I was twenty-three. I wasn't a kid. Anyway. My point is, I swore I'd never do that to a family of my own."

"Deacon."

"I know that's irrational. Statistically, I'll live into my fifties and beyond. But that's just always been on my mind."

"So, what are you saying?"

"I'm saying, just like my vow to never marry, my vow to not have children is based on a fear that first manifested in the mind of a twenty-three-year-old who was suddenly thrust into being the head of the family."

"So...what are you saying?"

"I'm saying in a very long-winded way I'd like to have children."

"You want to have babies with me?"

"That'd probably be the best way to do it. I mean, having them with someone else might be frowned upon. But if you insist—"

She kissed him. "You really want to have a family?"

"Yes. I really want to have a family."

She smiled and teared up. "I didn't want to pressure you. But that makes me really, really happy."

"I don't want to have them like nine months from now."

"Of course not."

"But maybe we could start thinking about it in a year or so."

She nodded. "That sounds perfect."

He moved some hair from her neck and kissed her. "Of course, in the meantime, we could work on the process, so when we're ready we'll be experts."

"That sounds like a really good plan."

"Well, I like to be prepared."

"Yes, you do."

He pushed her back onto the bed and kissed her.

She giggled and looked at him. "We're supposed to be at dinner in thirty minutes."

"No problem." He kissed her again. "Actually, we might be a tad late."

"You know Ruthie hates it when we're late for dinner."

"Ruthie will just have to deal."

Chapter Thirteen

"It's a friggin' slumber party."

When Deacon and Cassidy came into the dining room fifteen minutes late for dinner, Tobias looked at his brother and knew exactly what they'd been up to.

"Glad you could make it."

Deacon pulled out Cassidy's chair before sitting down. Ruthie appeared in the doorway with her hands on her hips and Deacon looked at her.

"Sorry, Ruthie."

She harrumphed, then left the room while Cassidy served them both some spaghetti. Deacon grabbed a roll and picked up his fork.

"This looks great. I'm starving."

Tobias grinned. "I bet you are." He took a drink from his iced tea. "So, family ride tomorrow, then what?"

Cassidy smiled at him. "Guy's night out. Girls' night in."

"Oh, shit." He glanced at Riley and covered his mouth. "Dang, how'd I forget about the bachelor party?"

Deacon nodded. "Yeah, best man. How did you forget about that?" He glanced at Gemma. "Must have other stuff on your mind."

Gemma took a second piece of bread. "So what does a Carmichael brother's bachelor party look like? Alcohol? Dancing girls?"

Tobias laughed. "This is for Deacon. Yes, on the booze. No, on the girls."

"Of course. Where are you going?"

"We're camping out. We have a spot on the other side of the valley. It's at the tail end of Washburn Lake. Real pretty spot."

"And who's going?"

Tobias looked around the table. "Just the three of us."

"So, it's a brother's camp out?"

He shook his head. "Don't make it sound so lame. It's going to be cool."

"I'm sure."

Abby laughed. "Sounds super cool."

Tobias frowned at her. "Shut up."

Tanner smiled. "Sounds cool to me." He looked at Deacon. "Do I get to drink?"

"We'll bring plenty of soft drinks for you, kid."

"That's not what I meant."

Deacon looked at Preston. "It just occurred to me we've been leaving you out a bit, Preston."

"Oh no. That's fine. I'm a guest. I'm not in the wedding party. Or a friend of anybody. I'm just Gemma's plus one."

Deacon glanced at Gemma. "I'm sure you're more than that. You should join us tomorrow night."

Tobias stretched his leg out to kick Deacon under the table, but Deacon had anticipated the move and tucked his feet under his chair.

Deacon looked at Tobias. "Right, Tobias?"

"Um...sure. The more the merrier." He aggressively took a bite of spaghetti. "Do you play poker?"

"A little, yeah."

Gemma shook her head. "He plays fairly regularly. And he's pretty good, from what I've heard."

Preston shrugged.

Deacon nodded. "Then it's settled. You'll come with us."

"Do I have to ride a horse?"

"No. There's a road. It's all very civilized, with tents, beds, chairs, lots of food and beverages, and a large firepit. All with a beautiful view of the lake."

Preston nodded. "Okay. Thank you. I appreciate the invite."

Riley looked at Gemma. "What am I going to do?"

"You get to hang out with us women."

"Aww."

"It'll be fun."

Abby smiled at him. "Lots of good snacks. We might even play a game or two. And you get to stay up late."

Riley smiled. "Okay. I'm in."

Abby looked at Deacon. "You know who else would love to come to your bachelor camp-out?"

"Who?"

Tobias shook his head. "Oh no. No Harvard men allowed."

"Stop with the stupid college rivalry." She looked at Preston. "Where did you go to college?"

"Stanford."

"Great. We'll throw another school into the ring."

Deacon pushed his plate aside. "What makes you think Skyler wants to come with us?"

"He doesn't have many friends here. His parents still keep a tight leash on him even though he's twenty-three now. A night out will do him good. And they can't have a problem with him hanging out with the Carmichael brothers." She glanced at Preston. "And friend."

Deacon shrugged. "Sure. He can come."

"I'll call him after dinner." She looked at Tobias. "Now, I want to hear why you came home from your trail ride wet."

"I told you Riley and I waded in the creek."

"You were all wet." She stuck out her lower lip. "Did you fall?"

Riley raised his hand and started laughing. "I did. I slipped. I fell right on my butt."

"Oh my goodness."

Gemma patted Riley's arm. "And then Tobias decided to join him. So he sat right down in the water next to Riley."

Riley was still laughing. "Then we went under. It was really cold."

Tobias nodded. "*Really* cold."

Riley looked around Gemma to see Tobias. "Then Tobias picked up Mom and took her to the water." He leaned back in his chair, laughing uncontrollably.

Preston looked at Gemma and then at Tobias. "You picked her up and dropped her in the creek?"

Tobias sat straighter in his chair. "No. I didn't drop her in the water. I was just teasing her."

"But you carried her to the water?"

Gemma smiled at Preston. "It was all in fun. No harm."

Deacon cleared his throat. "Okay. Sounds like a fun afternoon. Anyone care to join Cassidy and me for a walk before it gets too dark?"

Gemma looked around the table. "I'll come."

Preston nodded at her. "I'll keep an eye on Riley."

Abby stood. "I've got a phone call to make."

Tanner got to his feet as well. "Me too."

Tobias shook his head. "Ah, young love."

Abby frowned at him. "Skyler and I are friends."

"Oh, right. Of course."

Gemma was walking beside Cassidy and Deacon. They'd taken off across the pasture behind the barn. "I must say, this is the most beautiful place I've ever been."

Cassidy nodded. "Isn't it great?"

"How long has your family lived here, Deacon?"

"Four generations."

"My goodness. Tobias showed me the house he's building. He said you were originally going to build there."

"Yeah." He put his arm around Cassidy. "It was going to be my bachelor pad. Fortunately, I kept dragging my feet. It was more convenient to stay here. Then I met Cassidy. And everything changed."

"So, you'll be staying in the family home?"

"Yes. Abby will find a husband someday, heaven forbid. Tanner will be away at school soon. I need to be there for our mother."

"Of course. Who's this Skyler? Is he a prospect for Abby?"

Cassidy smiled. "He is from a very wealthy family. The only child. His parents have high aspirations for him."

Deacon shook his head. "Poor kid. I get the feeling he's more interested in Abby than Abby is in him."

Cassidy took his arm. "I don't understand that. Skyler is really cute. And seems like a nice kid."

Deacon looked at her. "Kid? You're only two and a half years older than him."

"Yeah. But I'm about to be a married woman. That makes me years older than him."

"How so?"

She shrugged. "I don't know. Twenty-five just seems a lot older than twenty-three."

"You're making me feel ancient."

Gemma laughed. "How old is Tobias?"

"He just turned twenty-seven. And I know he seems so much younger than that."

———————— ❧ ————————

When she got back to her room, Gemma went in to spend some time with Riley and Preston before bedtime. She could tell Preston was still brooding about Tobias carrying her to the creek. He wasn't jealous necessarily. Or maybe he was. She wasn't sure. It was probably more about the fact Tobias carried her at all. Preston had never done anything so overtly masculine in their entire two-year relationship. She smiled thinking about it, and Preston frowned at her.

"What are you smiling about?"

"Nothing in particular. I'm just happy. I'm having a great time."

He sighed. "I'll be glad to get back to the city."

Of course he will. She looked at Riley. "How about you? Are you having a good time?"

He nodded enthusiastically. "I love it here. I never want to leave."

"I suppose you don't." She looked at Preston. "You really should try to enjoy yourself a little more."

"Well, apparently I'm camping tomorrow night. Super fun."

Gemma stood and picked up Riley. "Come on, kid, you get to sleep with me tonight. Preston is being a grumpy puss."

Preston frowned at her again. "Whatever."

She took Riley into her room and settled him into her bed, then gave him her phone to play games on while she took a shower.

"When I come out, it's bedtime."

"Okay."

She came out of the bathroom thirty minutes later and Riley was playing Candy Crush. She sat next to him and leaned against some pillows resting on the headboard.

Riley looked at her. "Do you want a turn?"

"Yeah. Hand it over."

They played for twenty minutes until they ran out of lives, then it was time for bed for Riley.

"Okay, mister. Bedtime."

He handed her the phone and snuggled into the blankets. "Mom?"

"Yes, honey."

"Can we stay here forever?"

She brushed some hair out of his eyes. "I wish we could. I really do. But I have my job to go to. And you have school."

"Not till summer's over. Besides, I could go to school here."

"Wouldn't you miss your friends?"

He shrugged. "Maybe a little. But I can make new friends. I already have a new friend. Tobias."

"He is a good friend, huh?"

"Yeah. He's the best."

Gemma nodded. She had to agree. "Okay. Close your eyes. I'll leave this one light on so I can read." She kissed him. "Sleep tight. Love you."

"Love you, too."

Riley had a busy day, and it didn't take long for him to fall asleep. Gemma tried to get into the book she brought, but she couldn't concentrate. All she could think about was Tobias. He'd picked her up like it was nothing. And every time she thought about it, her stomach did a little flip-flop. It was really hard being so close to someone and then just turn it off and pretend it didn't happen. It did happen. That night in Malady Springs was real. And wonderful. At least she'd always have the memory of that.

She was still trying to read at eleven when her phone rang. She answered it quickly, so the sound didn't wake Riley.

"Hello?"

"Hey. Did I wake you?"

"Tobias? No. How'd you get my phone number?"

"You sent me the pictures you took today."

"Oh, right."

"Is it okay I called?"

She set her book aside. "Yes. I was just reading a book that isn't very good, so thank you for the interruption."

"I'm here to help."

"I'm not complaining, but why are you calling, Tobias?"

She heard him sigh. "I just wanted to hear your voice."

She smiled. "You're very sweet. You know that?"

"A few people have mentioned it. Mostly old ladies, but..."

"I bet you are sweet to old ladies."

He laughed. "I'm a couple of rums in so I'm going to say something I shouldn't."

"What's that?"

"Stay."

She was quiet for a moment. "Tobias."

"I know. I'll hate myself tomorrow for saying it. But it's how I feel."

She knew she had to change the subject. "Tell me about your family trail ride tomorrow."

"Okay. Sharp right turn away from the tipsy guy's inappropriate statement."

"It sounds like it's a semi-regular thing."

"Me being tipsy or inappropriate?"

"The trail ride."

"Oh, right. We go on Christmas if there's not too much snow. And birthdays. Also the 4th of July because it was my dad's favorite holiday."

"And where do you go?"

"We go to the north side of the property where it meets the forest service land. There's a big twisty oak where we scattered our father's ashes."

She sat up. "Oh my goodness. I didn't know. I'm sorry."

"You've got nothing to be sorry for. It's not a secret. And it's not a depressing trip. We have fun and enjoy each other's company. Then we toast Dad, and fill him in on what we've been up to."

She laid back down. "It sounds nice."

"It is. It's how we stay connected to him."

She put a hand on Riley when he stirred in his sleep. "And tomorrow night is your slumber party."

"Slumber party? No way. It's totally not a slumber party. What you're doing is a slumber party."

"Okay. Calm down. I just thought it didn't sound all that different from what we women are doing. Spending the night, a little drinking, eating junk food, gossiping."

"Shit. It's a friggin' slumber party."

Gemma laughed. "I'm sure it's much more manly than ours will be."

"There are some differences. We'll be drinking a lot, and grilling steaks. And instead of gossiping, we'll be swapping stories of...manly stuff and shit like that."

"I stand corrected."

"I should hope so."

Chapter Fourteen

"Geez, Dad. Did I miss curfew?"

Tobias was in the kitchen with a cup of coffee when Deacon came in the back door.

"What the hell? Are you hungover?"

"No. I'm good."

"We've been ready to leave for a half-hour."

"Sorry, I'm coming." He finished his coffee.

Ruthie held out a banana and a muffin. Tobias took the muffin and frowned at the banana. "What the hell am I supposed to do with that?"

"It's good for you."

He held up the muffin. "So is this."

Deacon went out the door, and Tobias followed him. "I swear. I'm not hungover. I was up late."

"Why? And how late?"

"Jeez, Dad. Did I miss curfew?" Deacon glanced at Tobias and he went on. "I was talking to Gemma on the phone. We talked until two. Or something like that."

Deacon stopped walking. "Well, shit. That sounds serious."

Tobias passed him and kept walking. "Let's get this show on the road."

Tanner and Abby were already on their horses when they got to the front of the barn. Tobias and Deacon mounted theirs, and the four of them took off across the field. Tobias lagged behind while he took a bite of his muffin.

Abby slowed down and waited for him. "You look tired."

"I'm fine." He was tired. But the lack of sleep was totally worth it. He and Gemma had talked about a lot of random stuff. Nothing too important, but he learned a lot about her. He was beginning to get a sense of who she was, and he liked it.

"I talked to Skyler. He's totally stoked to go tonight."

"Awesome, *dude*."

She laughed. "You act like you don't like him. But I know you do."

"He's okay, for a—"

She pointed at him. "Don't say it."

"I was going to say for a rich kid."

"You're a rich kid. We're all rich kids."

"I know. But he's different rich than we are. He's a spoiled rich kid."

"He is not."

Tobias glanced at her. "It's not his fault. He has parents who fawn over him and give him whatever he wants. We have Deacon."

"That's not very nice. Deacon did fine."

"I agree. I'm not dissing him. I'm glad we grew up knowing what really matters. Other than the whole Yale thing. Deacon did right by us." He truly meant it. Without Deacon he didn't know where they'd all be or what would've happened to The Starlight.

"He is overly obsessed with college."

"Yeah. But it was a semi-interesting adventure."

"Maybe for you. I'm not finding it interesting at all."

"I'm sorry. Do you want me to talk to Deacon over the summer? Try to get him to back off a little?"

"Please."

"Okay. I'll talk. But he probably won't listen."

Tobias finished his muffin and they broke into a trot to catch up with Tanner and Deacon.

When they came to a long stretch of grassland about two miles across, Tobias stopped his horse. "Hold up." The others stopped. "Anybody interested in a little race to the trees?"

Tanner grinned. "Hell, yeah."

"Okay. On three. One, two—" Tobias dug his heels into Chance's side and the horse took off. Deacon cursed and started after him, with Tanner and Abby right behind them.

They all raced across the field at a full gallop and Abby pulled ahead at the last minute and stopped short of the trees.

She took off her hat and waved it over her head. "You all are so slow. I even beat the cheater."

Tobias laughed. "I didn't cheat."

"You went on two."

"Did I? Huh. I guess I counted wrong."

Deacon scowled at Tobias, then looked at Abby. "Good ride, Abigale."

Tanner shook his head. "Man, I almost caught you."

She smiled. "Your cow pony isn't built for speed, I guess."

Deacon started his horse walking and headed for the trees. "Okay. Let's go slow and easy the rest of the way."

They arrived at the old oak tree an hour later and dismounted. They tied the horses to nearby trees, then went to the large, twisted oak.

Abby sighed. "Hi, Dad."

Deacon put his arm around her and she laid her head on his shoulder. Tobias came up beside them with a bottle of bourbon. He held it up, then opened it and took a sip. He passed it off to Deacon, who drank some, then looked at Abby. She took it from him and took a tiny sip, then made a face and handed it to Tanner. He looked at Deacon and got a nod, then took a drink. He coughed, and Tobias grinned as he took the bottle and put the lid back on.

He looked at Deacon. "You should go first. You've got the biggest news to share."

Deacon nodded and got down from his horse, He handed the reins to Tobias, then walked toward the tree, while the other three moved far enough away to give him some privacy.

When Deacon joined them ten minutes later, Tobias headed for the tree. He sat on a large root and took his hat off.

"I don't have a lot to say. Not too much going on. I do wish I could get some advice from you, though." He set his hat on the grass. "I met this girl." He smiled. "I know what you're thinking. Not again. But this one. Damn. She's special. Like now and forever, special." He was quiet for a moment while he thought about Gemma. "But like everything else, it's complicated. I won't bore you with the details, but trust me, it's going to be an uphill battle. I'm not sure how it's going to turn out. But maybe when I see you next, I'll have some news. Hopefully, it'll be good news." He put his hat back on and got to his feet. "I love you, Dad. And I miss the hell out of you."

Abby and Tanner both took their turns at the tree, then they all sat to eat the picnic lunch Ruthie had packed for them.

Halfway through his sandwich, Tobias glanced at Deacon. "So, two more days of being single."

"Yep. I'm ready."

"Yeah. I imagine you are."

Tanner smiled. "Who's going to be next?"

Tobias looked at him. "Probably you. You just need to decide which Wexler sister you want to marry."

"I'm not getting married for a really long time."

"Okay. Whatever."

"And if I was. It'd be Hallie, of course."

"Right." Tobias glanced at Abby. "Maybe you'll be next."

"Me? I don't even have any prospects. Which is fine, by the way. I'm not looking to be anyone's wife anytime soon."

Deacon shook his head. "Yeah. You just wait. I thought the same thing. Then lightning strikes and everything changes."

Tobias thought about Gemma again, and Deacon looked at him. "Right, Tobias?"

"I wouldn't know."

"I'm pretty sure you do."

Tanner looked at the two of them. "What am I missing?" He set his sandwich down. "I knew something was going on. Why doesn't anyone ever tell me anything?"

Tobias patted his shoulder. "It's nothing, kid."

Abby shook her head. "It's not nothing. Tobias has the hots for Gemma."

Tobias pointed a finger at her. "Wow. Nice way to put it."

"Well, it's true." She looked at Tanner. "Don't worry. Nothing improper is going on. Gemma isn't really with Preston. They came to the wedding together because Riley wanted Preston to come."

Tanner thought for a moment. "But they used to be together?"

"Yeah. But not anymore."

"Good. I don't really like that guy. He's kind of a douche."

Tobias nodded. "Now that, I agree with."

"So, you and she are...?"

"Just friends. She's going back to Austin in a few days. Nothing else we can be."

"Well, that's a bummer."

"Yeah. It's a bummer alright."

Deacon got to his feet. "It'll all work out."

Tobias stood, too. "Quit saying that. Just because it all worked out for you and Cassidy. It doesn't mean it will work out for me and Gemma. You only had me standing in your way. Gemma and I have eight hours and a career between us."

Tanner looked up at him. "Eight hours isn't that far. Not if you really want to see someone."

"Can we change the subject please?"

Tanner stood. "No. Why is it such a big deal? You could go see her. She could come see you. If you really want it to work, it could."

"That's no way to have a relationship. I want to wake up every morning with her, not drive eight hours to go spend a weekend with her."

"Sometimes, you gotta take what you can get."

Tobias went to Chance and tightened the cinch on his saddle. "We should get back. Guys night out starts in a few hours." He mounted Chance. "Are you coming?"

Deacon went to his horse. "Yeah, Tobias, we're coming."

When they got back to the ranch, Tanner and Abby put the horses away while Deacon and Tobias headed for the house. Deacon went to the dining room, where Ruthie and Cassidy were working on the seating chart.

Tobias went to the den and poured himself a rum, then set the balls up on the pool table. He'd sunk half of them when Gemma came into the room.

"How was the ride?"

"It was great."

"How's your leg?"

"A little stiff. But tolerable." He smiled at her. "Do you play pool?"

"I play at pool. I'm not good at it. At all. I'm terrible."

He handed her his cue. "Let me see you hit a couple of balls." He watched her attempt to sink a ball, but after she missed the pocket twice, he laughed. "You weren't kidding. You are terrible. I thought maybe you were just trying to hustle me."

"No. Afraid not. This is it. This is me playing pool."

He took the cue from her and sunk the rest of the balls.

She put her hands on her hips. "Well, aren't you a showoff?"

"Unlike you, I'm damn good at pool."

"I see that."

He started collecting the balls to rack them up again. "I had a talk with my dad about you today."

"That's sweet."

"Yeah. He didn't have much to say. But Tanner told me if I wanted it bad enough, I'd make it happen."

"Hmm. That's not always as easy as it sounds."

"I tried to tell him that, but he's young. And idealistic."

"Right."

Tobias leaned on the cue and looked at her. "What the hell am I going to do about you?"

She studied him for a moment. "You're going to let me go in a few days. And you're going to forget about me. And you're going to move on with your life."

He shook his head. "No. Wrong answer. I think I like the young idealist's take better." He went to the end of the table, took aim, and sent the racked balls flying around the table. "Come over here. I'm going to give you a pool lesson."

"I think it's hopeless."

"Nothing is hopeless."

Chapter Fifteen

"All's fair in love, war, and poker."

The camp where the bachelor party was being held was used for various things. It was quite elegant by cowboy standards, with six canvas tents large enough for a double bed and a small dresser and two chairs. There was also a permanent bathroom with a flushable toilet, a shower stall, and a sink. The kitchen was also in a permanent building with a refrigerator, a gas stove, and a cupboard stocked with non-perishables. There was a generator to run the hot water heater, refrigerator, and the lights strung across the open area in front of the tents. The camp also had its own well to supply water.

It was located on an arm of Washburn Lake, which was partially on Carmichael land. They'd secured the water rights to the lake fifty years ago, which added a nice sum to their yearly income. Any ranch that needed to use lake water for crops or livestock had to buy it from the Carmichaels.

Tobias smiled at Preston and Skyler's reaction when they saw the camp.

"Not what you were expecting?"

Preston shook his head. "No. Not at all."

Skyler nodded. "I've heard about this place. My dad's been here a few times for your yearly rich guys' retreat."

Tobias put a hand on his shoulder. "Maybe someday when you grow up, you can come with your daddy."

Skyler ducked out of his grasp. "No thanks. Bachelor party, yes. Retreat? Nah."

Some of the ranch hands had stocked the camp, got the tents set up and ready, and swept the ground around the area. It was perfect and pristine. Deacon took his bag out of the back of his Jeep. "I'm going to claim the tent closest to the lake."

"Go for it, brother. It's your night, after all."

The others all put their stuff in their chosen tent, then gathered at the large firepit. When Deacon prepared to get the fire going, Tobias stopped him.

"No work for the groom. Let me."

Deacon looked at him. "You know I like to build the fire."

"Fine. Build away."

"Thank you."

Tanner laughed. "I'm going to go check out the lake." He looked at Skyler. "Want to come with?"

"Sure."

They headed for the lake and Tobias looked at Preston, who seemed a little uptight.

"Dude, relax."

Preston nodded. "Sorry. This is all a little foreign to me."

"Luxury camping?"

"Uh...all of it. You guys live in a whole different world than I do."

"Embrace it. You only live once."

"Yeah. Of course." He glanced toward Tanner and Skyler. "I'll go check out the lake with them."

"Sounds like a plan."

He waited until Preston was out of hearing range, then went to Deacon. "Why the hell did you invite him?"

Deacon laughed. "He does seem a bit like a duck out of water."

"He's going to be a killjoy. He's going to ruin everything."

"Give it time. And some alcohol. He'll loosen up."

Tobias pointed at him. "Alcohol. That's the ticket."

By the time Tanner, Skyler, and Preston came back from the lake, Deacon had a nice fire going and Tobias had the large propane barbecue warming up. He looked at the other men.

"Who wants steak?"

Everyone raised their hand.

"Okay. Coming right up." He nodded toward an ice chest. "There's beer for those of us who are legal, and soft drinks for you, Tanner."

Tanner frowned at Deacon. "Really? You're not even going to let me drink at your bachelor party?"

"You can have a beer with your steak. And maybe one later when we bring out the cards."

Tanner smiled. "Cool, thanks."

Tobias grilled up the steaks, then brought them to the big redwood picnic table where everyone was seated. The steaks were accompanied by a green salad and a potato salad Ruthie had sent along. She also sent two apple pies and a tray of brownies for dessert.

When he was done with his steak, Deacon cut into the pie. "Ruthie, I love you."

Tobias laughed. "Yeah. Even when I move into my house, I'm going to be dropping in for dinner, a lot."

"You're always welcome. My house is literally your house, as well."

Preston took a bite of a brownie. "Gemma said you showed her your house."

"Yeah. It's just a frame now. But I hope to get it done over the summer and move in before winter sets in."

"Hmm."

Tanner shook his head. "You're going to be lonely."

"Nah. Besides, it's thirty minutes away by horse."

Preston looked at him. "You can only get to it by horse?"

"No. there's a road. It's just quicker by horse."

Skyler drank some beer. "I spent the winter upgrading the original homestead on our ranch. I had to get out of my father's house."

Deacon nodded. "I've been in that house. It's nice. Four bedrooms?"

"Yeah. I know. Kind of big for a single guy. But if my parents get their way, I won't be single for long."

Tobias laughed. "Stay strong. Don't let them rope you into anything you don't want to do."

"With my parents, that's easier said than done."

Tobias looked at Deacon. "Thank you, brother."

"For what?"

"For only being a hard ass about college. You've left my love life alone."

"Hmm. Sometimes I wonder if I shouldn't have married you off a few years ago."

"Never gonna happen."

Tanner smiled. "Yeah. That's what Deacon said up until last September."

Preston looked at Deacon. "You've only been engaged since September?"

"No. I met Cassidy in September. September fifteenth. Actually, I met her a few days before that. But we don't count that. I asked her to marry me on Thanksgiving Day."

"Wow. That was quick."

Tobias grinned. "It's the fireworks man. They'll get you every time." He noted Preston's confusion and was quite happy the man had no idea what he was talking about.

After dinner, it was time to bring out the cards and the hard liquor. They brought a bottle each of scotch, rum, and bourbon. Each man poured a shot of their drink of choice, while Tanner enjoyed his second beer.

They decided on Five-Card Stud and used chips to bet with. They wanted to keep it friendly. Using actual money would only lead to trouble. As Gemma had said, Preston was pretty good. Skyler was only fair. And Tanner did surprisingly well. But he grew up playing with his brothers. Deacon seemed to have the most luck and won a majority of the hands.

When it was his turn as dealer, he shuffled the cards. "I don't know if I'm this good, or if you all are taking it easy on me."

Tobias laughed. "All's fair in love, war, and poker. You have lady luck with you tonight."

"Hmm. Okay."

Preston had lost a few hands in a row and when he saw his new cards, he swore and dropped them on the table.

Tobias smiled at him. "Everything okay there, Preston?"

"It's great. Just great."

"It's a friendly game, man. No room for temper tantrums."

Preston scowled at him. "I'm not throwing a tantrum. I'd just like to get a decent hand once in a while. Everyone else is getting decent hands. Me? I get shit cards."

"Whoa. What are you saying?"

Deacon cleared his throat. "Tobias. Let the man be."

Tobias shook his head. "It sounds to me like he's saying we're dealing him bad cards on purpose. That we're cheating."

"That's not what he said." Deacon looked at Preston. "Right? That's not what you meant?"

Preston took a breath. "No. Of course not."

Tanner stood up. "I'm going to go grab some chips. Tobias, you want to come help me?"

Tobias looked at him. "You need help carrying chips?"

"Just come on."

Tobias stood and followed Tanner into the kitchen.

Tanner took his arm. "Chill out, man."

"Me chill out? The guy's a prick."

"I agree. But let's not get into a brawl at Deacon's bachelor party. Especially when it really has nothing to do with cards."

"What are you saying?"

"He's jealous of you spending time with his ex-girlfriend. You're jealous of him because he's Gemma's ex-boyfriend."

"That's not what this is." Tanner cocked his head and Tobias sighed. "Okay, fine. That's exactly what it is."

"So, chill. She left him. She's hanging out with you."

Tobias took a moment. "So, I win?"

"Exactly."

Tobias slapped him on the back. "When did you get so smart?"

"I've always been smart. You just never chose to notice."

"I notice, kid. I notice. You're going to give Deacon a run for his money at Yale."

"Actually, I was thinking of applying to Harvard."

Tobias looked at him, then grabbed him and wrestled him to the ground. "Take that back, you traitor."

Tanner laughed. "Okay. I was kidding. I take it back."

When Skyler came in and saw them on the ground, he stopped walking and looked at them. "Are you guys okay in here?"

Tanner got up and held a hand out to Tobias. "Come on, old man."

He slapped Tanner's hand away and got to his feet. "I'm not the old man around here." He rubbed his left thigh. "I feel like it sometimes, though." He looked at Skyler. "Did you come to help us carry the bag of chips?"

Skyler laughed. "No, I came to tell you, Preston has excused himself for the night."

"Thank, God."

"I know. That guys a prick."

Tobias grinned. "I believe I'm starting to like you, Skyler. Even though you are a Harvard educated, Fremont."

"Thank you, Tobias. I might be able to overlook the fact you're a Yale man and a Carmichael."

Tanner laughed. "Come on guys. Let's go play some poker."

They left the kitchen and joined Deacon at the table. He looked at them as they all sat down. "You all three went into the kitchen for chips and you came back empty-handed."

The four of them played until after midnight, then sat around and talked until two. When Tobias wandered out of his tent at ten a.m., he laughed at the ragged men sitting around the firepit drinking coffee.

"How we doing this morning, gentlemen?"

"Deacon waved a hand at him. Don't talk so loudly."

"How come I'm the only one who isn't hungover?"

"Maybe because you are so much more experienced at drinking, than we are."

Tobias put a hand to his chest. "Ouch. That hurt a little bit."

Tanner came out of the kitchen with a muffin in his hand. "I'm not hungover."

Deacon scowled at him. "That's because you only had two beers."

Tanner shrugged and poured himself some coffee. "There are muffins in there. Some apple fritters. And a loaf of banana nut bread. Unless someone is going to cook up some bacon and eggs."

Deacon shook his head. "I think I'll pass."

Tobias sat next to Deacon. "So, one thing I don't understand. You didn't drink nearly as much last night as you did that night in Abilene. Yet you got up the next morning, snuck out of the hotel, paid the bill, bought a horse, borrowed a horse trailer, then took a four-hour trail ride. How'd you do that?"

"I was on a mission."

"Right, a fix things mission. Only halfway to the cabin, you realized you didn't want to fix it."

"Exactly. Which leads directly to this moment right here. I'm hungover the day before my wedding."

"As you should be."

Deacon laughed. "I wonder how the women fared."

Chapter Sixteen

"You really need to behave."

C assidy and Gemma met the men in the driveway when they heard the vehicles returning. When Gemma noticed Tobias and Preston weren't riding together, she got a little worried.

Tobias got out of Deacon's Jeep and smiled at her, then glanced at Preston when he got out of Tanner's truck. Preston thanked Deacon, before heading for Gemma.

"I'll be in the room. I need to shower."

"Okay. How was it?"

"It was not what I expected."

"Is that good or bad?"

He didn't answer her and continued on into the house. Gemma raised her eyebrows at Tobias, who shrugged. He seemed to be a little stiff, and he was favoring his leg.

Deacon looked at him. "Go sit. Tanner and I have this." Cassidy came to him and gave him a hug and a kiss, while Skyler walked to the back of the truck.

"I can help."

Tobias nodded. "Thanks. But sitting is not what I need. I need to walk."

Gemma smiled. "Do you want some company?"

"Sure."

She joined him and they headed down the path toward the pond. Riley came out of the house and ran down the stairs. "Can I come with?"

"Of course, honey. I thought you were helping Ruthie."

"I was, but I want to walk with you guys."

Tobias patted Riley's head. "Come on. Have you seen the pond yet?"

"There's a pond?"

"Yeah. Run ahead if you want, but stop when you see the water."

"Okay."

Gemma called after him. "Listen to what Tobias said. Don't get near the water."

"I won't."

She looked at Tobias. "How big is this pond?"

"Pretty big."

"So, how'd it go? Was Preston civil?"

"Um...for a while. He got a little pissed when the cards didn't go in his favor."

"Oh no. I'm sorry."

Tobias looked at her. "It's not your fault. You're not responsible for his attitude."

"Maybe. But I brought him with me."

"Yeah. You did, didn't you?"

She glanced at him. "Tobias."

"Sorry, I still don't understand you and him. It doesn't make sense."

She took his arm. "I was trying to be responsible. I was trying to do the right thing for Riley."

"By dating a..." Tobias cleared his throat. "Sorry, again. None of my business."

They reached the pond and Riley had stopped six feet away, as he'd been told.

He turned to them as they approached. "Can I go by the water now?"

Gemma nodded. "Don't get wet."

"Okay."

"I'm serious, Riley."

"Okay, Mom."

Gemma looked at Tobias. "He's so happy here."

"It's pretty much a kid's paradise."

They sat next to each other on a bench and watched Riley run around, chase ducks, and throw rocks into the water. Tobias stretched out his leg and rubbed his thigh.

Gemma sighed. "Preston was safe. He was stable. He had a good job. It wasn't the most exciting relationship, but he treated me good."

"Okay. I get it. You have a kid. You can't be doing crazy stuff like...picking up cowboys in a bar." He glanced at her.

"You are pretty much everything Preston isn't."

"Hold on. I'm stable. I have a good job. And if given the chance, I'd treat you really good."

"I guess I was referring to the exciting part."

"You find me exciting?"

"To the point of distraction, yes. Despite what you may think, I don't make a habit of picking up cowboys in bars. I don't even make a habit of going to bars."

He grinned. "You just couldn't resist me, right?"

"Something like that."

Tobias leaned towards her and nudged her. "Well, despite the fact I'm going to be heartbroken in a couple of days when you leave. I'm damn glad you walked into the bar."

"I am too. And I wish there was some way to avoid the heart-break part."

"There is. Don't go."

"Time to change the subject."

Tobias got to his feet with a small groan. "Riley. Do you know how to skip stones?"

Riley shook his head.

"Well, it's about time you learned."

Gemma watched Tobias patiently teach Riley how to skip stones into the pond for the next thirty minutes. Tobias was really good with him. Maybe because he was a bit of a child himself. But she liked that about him. Life with Tobias would be fun and interesting. She stopped herself. Life with Tobias would involve giving up her life in Austin. Her career. Moving away from friends and family. The family wasn't that big of an issue. Although her parents had proven to be better grandparents than they were parents.

Tobias looked at her. "Come join us."

"I'm not very good."

"I don't care."

She went to them and he handed her a flat, round stone. "Just chuck it in there."

She threw the stone, which hit and sunk.

Tobias laughed. "Okay. Perhaps I used the wrong word. By chuck, I meant toss it with finesse." He picked up another stone and threw it in angling from the side. "Kind of like throwing a Frisbee only backwards."

Gemma laughed. "I can't throw a Frisbee either."

Tobias looked at her. "So, you can't play pool. You can't throw a Frisbee. What can you do? You know, sports related. You are quite good at a couple of things."

She shook her head and glanced at Riley. "I can play horseshoes."

"Really? Well, that's something. We happen to have a horseshoe pit out behind the house."

"You do?"

"Yes. No one uses it because horseshoes are so lame. But maybe tomorrow you can show me what you've got."

"So you can make fun of me?"

"I'd never."

"Seeing as tomorrow is your brother's wedding. We might not find the time to do that."

"Oh shit. The wedding's tomorrow."

"Yes. And the rehearsal dinner is in a couple of hours. So we probably should get back."

"Okay. Let's go." He tossed one last stone, skipping it four times before it dropped into the water. "Come on, kid, time to head back. I've got a speech to write."

Gemma looked at him. "You haven't written your best man speech yet?"

"I have for the wedding. Just not for tonight. I didn't know until a couple of days ago I had to say something nice tonight. I used up all the nice things I had to say on the wedding day toast."

She laughed. "I'm sure you'll do fine." She watched him walk. "Would you like a massage when we get back?"

He grinned at her. "More than you know."

"You really need to behave."

"I'm behaving. I'm a gentleman."

"Hmm."

He leaned in close to her. "Who came knocking on my door in Malady Springs? I'd said goodnight. I was ready to call it a night. Then..."

She punched him in the shoulder.

"Now I'll need you to massage my arm, too."

───────◦✦◦───────

Tobias had stepped out of the shower when he heard a knock on his door. He wrapped a towel around his waist, then went to the door and said, "Gemma?"

"Yes."

He opened the door a few inches.

She covered her eyes. "Tobias. You're not dressed."

"I knew I forgot something." He opened the door. "Come on in."

"Not until you're dressed."

He took her elbow and pulled her into the room, while she kept a hand over her eyes.

He laughed. "Seriously?"

"Please get dressed."

"Aren't you just going to ask me to take my pants back off?"

"You can leave your pants off. But please, put on underwear and a t-shirt."

He headed for the bathroom and when he glanced back, he saw she'd lowered her hand. He pointed at her. "Gemma Stone. I think you need to behave."

She pointed at the bathroom. "Get dressed."

He came back out in his boxers and a t-shirt. "Better?"

"No. But more appropriate. Lay down on the bed."

"Yes, ma'am."

"Stop or I'm going to leave."

He laid down on his side and she sat next to him. "You're not nearly as irresistible as you think you are."

"Yet you knocked on my door in Malady Springs."

"I was slightly intoxicated. And... Alright fine. You're somewhat irresistible."

"Thank you. So are you. Would you like to strip down to your boxers?"

She started massaging his thigh. "You're all tied up in knots again."

"The beds in the tents aren't very comfortable. I tossed and turned all night."

"You had beds?"

"Of course. It was all quite civilized." He closed his eyes for a moment. What she was doing was a combination of pain and relief. But it felt good in a weird way. "How was your slumber party?"

"It was really fun. Abby had a lot of Deacon and Tobias stories for us."

He grunted. "Great."

"She said you have a tendency to fall in love quite easily."

He lifted his head and looked at her. "That was the old me. After Cassidy, I gave up on that. I'm much more careful now."

"You were in love with Cassidy?"

"Well, not really. I could've fallen in love with her, though."

"I can see that. Cassidy is special. She and Deacon are really good together."

"Yep."

"Are you sorry it didn't work out between you and her?"

He laid his head back down. "No. Not at all. I wouldn't have met you."

She sighed. "Tobias."

"What?"

"That night in Malady Springs was the best and the worst night of my life."

He took a moment. "I know exactly what you mean."

She stayed another fifteen minutes, then left to go get ready for the rehearsal and the dinner following it.

Tobias put on a gray dress shirt but left it open at the collar. He had no plans to wear a tie. He paired it with black jeans and a black leather jacket. He put on his black ostrich boots and called it all good.

He still hadn't written anything down for his toast. He figured it'd come to him when the time came. Tanner and Abby were both going to speak tomorrow. But tonight it'd be just him and Gemma. It'd be a small group, just the six of them. And maybe their mother. Deacon had invited Ruthie too, but she said she wanted to save all her tears for the wedding.

Tobias was looking forward to spending an evening without Preston around. He was really getting tired of the guy. He grabbed his phone and wallet then headed downstairs. He found Deacon at their mother's door.

"Have you gone in yet?"

Deacon shook his head. "No. I'm kind of afraid of what I might find."

"Do you want me to go in?"

Deacon looked at him. "Would you mind?"

"Not at all. Go get yourself a shot of scotch. You're looking a little anxious."

Deacon nodded and headed for his office, while Tobias knocked on Faith's door, then opened it.

"Mother?"

She was on the bench by the window in a robe. Her hair was down, which it rarely was. She was still a young woman and quite beautiful. She looked at him.

"My, don't you look handsome."

"Thank you." He sat on the bench next to her. "Did you want to get dressed and come to dinner with us tonight?"

"Dinner with whom, dear?"

"Deacon, Tanner, Abby, Cassidy, and Gemma. And me, of course."

She patted his hand. "You go ahead. I'll wait here for your father."

Tobias sighed. "Okay, Mother." He got to his feet and kissed her cheek. "I love you."

"I love you too, sweetheart. Don't get into too much mischief."

"I won't."

He left the room, then went into Deacon's office. Deacon was leaning against his desk with a glass of scotch in his hand.

"What did she say?"

Tobias poured himself a shot of rum. "She's going to stay here and wait for Dad."

"Shit."

"I'm sorry, man."

Deacon shrugged. "I guess if she came, I'd be worrying about her all night."

"Still it sucks. I know. She was great until a couple of days ago."

"What do I tell her when she comes out of it and asks about the wedding?"

Tobias took a sip of rum. "If she comes out of it."

"You don't think she will?"

"It's been two days now."

"Shit."

Tobias patted Deacon's shoulder. "Go see Cassidy. I'll ask Ruthie to keep an eye on Mother."

Chapter Seventeen

"Saved by the Bible."

Tobias was waiting by the front door when Gemma came out of the guestrooms. She looked beautiful in a wispy light blue dress with tiny flowers on it. Her hair was up in a loose bun with tendrils of hair strategically released and hanging down her neck and in front of her ears.

Tobias nodded. "You look good enough to eat."

"Thank you. I think."

Deacon and Cassidy came down the stairs, along with Abby and Tanner. They all looked great as Carmichael's usually did. Deacon was dressed similarly to Tobias in charcoal slacks and a lighter gray shirt.

Tobias pointed at him. "And the Carmichael twins show up again."

Cassidy laughed. "You guys are going to have to start comparing notes before you get dressed to go out."

Abby put her arm through Tobias'. "Come on. You both look great. Let's not keep Pastor Joe waiting."

The wedding was taking place in the secret garden space at the Connelly house. It was going to be a small, informal ceremony with a few guests and family. The reception, with a lot more people, would take place in the main hall of the Connelly house, along with the flower gardens. Cassidy felt it was only fitting to marry Deacon in the spot she first met and fell in love with him.

When they entered the garden, Pastor Joe was standing on the small, raised platform built for the occasion.

"Evening, folks."

Deacon shook his hand. "Pastor Joe. Are we late?"

"No. Not at all. I got here early. I haven't been here in a while. I forgot how pretty it was."

He looked at the Greek statues, then smiled at Deacon.

Deacon shook his head. "I asked if they could remove them for the ceremony, but they said they weigh a ton."

The pastor looked at Cassidy. "I'm sure all eyes will be on the bride."

"That's for damn sure." Deacon put a hand to his mouth. "Sorry."

"Don't worry about it. I've been known to utter a curse word now and again."

Tobias laughed as he shook the pastor's hand. "Even so, we'll try to keep a lid on it."

Pastor Joe put everyone in their places, then went over the ceremony twice. When he asked if anyone had any questions, they all agreed they had it. The pastor thanked them and left, reminding them to be there by two tomorrow.

After he left, Gemma looked around the space. "This is great."

Cassidy came up to her. "Wait until you see it tomorrow. There are going to be flowers and candles."

Deacon stepped up to them. "Chairs."

Cassidy put a hand over his mouth. "A piano and a violinist."

Deacon removed her hand. "People."

She shook her head, then leaned in and kissed him.

He smiled. "Keep doing that. That'll shut me up."

Tobias walked over to a female statue and studied it for a moment. Gemma came up beside him, and he smiled at her.

"I took life drawing in college, and the female models didn't look anything like this."

"I didn't know you were an artist."

"I'm not."

She laughed. "Okay. I see where your mind was in college."

Deacon came up beside them. "I'm not so sure it's still not there."

Tobias shoved him. "Don't you have a bride to attend to?"

"You don't need to concern yourself with me and my bride. We're headed to the restaurant."

"If you take Abby, I'll catch a ride with Gemma." Tobias glanced at her and she nodded.

Deacon studied him for a moment. "Okay. Don't take too long admiring the statuary."

Tobias grinned. "Right behind you, brother."

He waited for them to leave, then smiled at Gemma. "I believe this is the first time I've had you to myself since...Malady Springs."

"What would you like to do about that?"

He took a step toward her, then stopped when Pastor Joe came through the entrance.

"Sorry folks, I left my Bible."

"No worries, Pastor." Tobias retreated a step from Gemma. "We'll see you tomorrow."

"Two o'clock. Make sure your brother gets here."

"I'm not too worried about Deacon getting cold feet."

The pastor smiled. "No. I guess not. Bye now."

Tobias watched him go, then looked at Gemma. "Saved by the Bible."

She took his hand. "It's just as well. Let's go eat."

Tobias sighed. "Doing the right thing really sucks."

They headed for her car. "In the long run, you'll be thankful for it."

"Eh. I don't think so. A little bit of regret is good for the character."

When they got to the car, she offered him the keys. "Would you like to drive?"

"Nah. I'm too depressed. I might be tempted to drive right off of the Black Creek bridge."

"Tobias, that's not funny."

"Sorry." He grinned at her. "It was a little funny, right?"

"No."

"Fine." He got into the passenger seat and buckled his seatbelt. "There have actually been three suicides off the bridge since it was built seventy-five years ago. Well, two confirmed. One might have had help going over."

"Oh my goodness."

"I'm full of trivia. If you want to know anything about Connelly or the Texas panhandle, I'm your man."

"Thank you. I'll keep that in mind." She turned the motor over. "Where are we going?"

"Take your next right, then left at the traffic light."

"The one and only traffic light?"

"Yeah. Can't miss it."

They arrived at the restaurant and when they went inside, they were directed to a large table in the back. Everyone else was there, and they took two seats across from each other. Deacon, Cassidy, and Gemma were on one side, and Tanner, Abby, and Tobias were on the other.

Tobias smiled at Deacon. "I thought this place closed down."

"Obviously not. The Sandersons took it over."

"Oh, right."

Gemma raised an eyebrow. "You know everything, huh?"

"Well, almost everything. More about past history than current affairs."

"Got it."

Tanner looked around Abby at Tobias. "He doesn't get out much."

"I like to stay home and do the work." He nodded toward Deacon. "He's the traveling man."

"Yeah, well, that's about to change."

"What do you mean?"

Deacon smiled. "It's time you start taking on some more responsibility."

"I'm plenty responsible. I manage the men and the day-to-day stuff. Despite the degree I was forced to get, I'm not the businessman in the family. You are." When Deacon continued to look at him, he said, "Shit. Seriously? Don't I have a say in this?"

Abby smiled. "Aww. He's going to share his mantle with you."

Tobias scowled. "Whatever."

Deacon put his arm around Cassidy. "I've got something to stay home for now."

"Yeah, yeah, I get it." He looked at Gemma. "See, if you'd just stay here and marry me, then we could send Tanner out on the road."

Abby frowned. "What about me? I could totally go do what Deacon does." Tobias and Deacon both looked at her. She shook her head. "I hate you guys."

Cassidy raised a hand. "Can I remind everyone why we're here? Deacon and I are getting married tomorrow. We're celebrating with our closest friends and family tonight."

Deacon kissed her. "She's right. No more business or ranch talk." He waved at the waitress. "Let's order some food."

Tobias pointed at him. "This conversation isn't over. To be continued at a later date."

"As soon as I get back from my honeymoon."

"Yeah. After that."

Everyone ordered what they wanted, and the food was all good. Tobias and Deacon had a little too much to drink, while the three women drank in moderation.

Deacon watched Abby sip from a glass of wine. "I still can't get used to you drinking."

"Three months now."

Gemma smiled at her. "And what do you think?"

Abby shrugged. "It's not nearly as fun as you think it's going to be when you're twenty and a half."

Tobias laughed. "You're just not doing it right." He got to his feet and tapped the rim of his empty glass with a knife. "Okay. Time for the obligatory toast."

Deacon shook his head. "It's not obligatory. I don't want to force you into toasting me."

"No, no. I got it." He cleared his throat and raised his glass, then frowned at it. "Hold on. There's supposed to be rum in my glass." He looked toward the bar. "I'll be right back." He left the table and returned a few minutes later with a double shot of rum. "Okay. Here we go. To my brother, the one and only Deacon Carmichael. I give you a hard time, and you give me a hard time. But I know, when times are really hard, you'll be there for me. And I believe I proved I'd be there for you that night in Abilene when I came across town at two in the morning to drag your drunk ass home. Although since you were at Kal El's hotel, you probably would've been okay."

Deacon laughed. "Even though you weren't speaking to me. You had my back."

"That's right. And you would've done the same for me."

"Damn right."

"So, I guess what I'm saying in this rum soaked toast is that I love you brother. And I love you, Cassidy. In a strictly brother-in-law way. Welcome to the family. And may you be blessed with a whole shitload of tiny little Carmichaels to carry on the family name." He raised his glass and took a drink.

Everyone else drank to the toast, and Tobias sat down and smiled at Gemma. "Who says you have to write a speech?"

She laughed. "You did good, Tobias."

"Thank you. Now it's your turn."

"Oh, right." She stood and lifted her glass of wine. "I met Cassidy in college when we were randomly placed in a dorm room together. We were instant friends, and we continued rooming together until I had to move back home, six years and nine months ago. We both had issues with our parents, and it was nice to have someone to commiserate with."

Tobias mumbled, "Boring."

Gemma pointed at him. "Shush. Anyway. When she called me last fall and told me she'd fallen for a cowboy. I couldn't quite believe it. But when she told me he wasn't just any old cowboy, he was pretty much *the* cowboy in northwestern Texas, it made a little more sense. And when I got here and met Deacon, and the rest of you. I understood there was no way she couldn't fall in love with all of you." She wiped a stray tear from her cheek and looked at Deacon. "I'm so glad she found you and your family. You've given her something she never really had." She raised her glass. "And that is all I can say. Or I'll start crying and I don't want to do that."

Everyone drank to her toast as she sat back down and Cassidy gave her a hug.

Tobias looked around the table. All three women had tears in their eyes. "Great. Three crying women. This is like my biggest nightmare."

Abby punched him in the shoulder.

He rubbed it. "Now I'm going to cry."

Deacon stood. "Hold on. One more. And I promise I'll try not to make you cry. We are a family. We're a strong family. A proud family. As individuals, we're not perfect. But as a family, we come pretty damn close. Tomorrow Cassidy officially becomes part of the family." He looked at Gemma. "And as the head of the Carmichael family, I'd like to extend an invitation. You and Riley are welcome anytime. After this week, you will forever be part of the family, too."

"How is that not supposed to make me cry?" She wiped her eyes. "Thank you Deacon. And none of us will bring up the fact that you left Preston out of the invitation."

Everyone laughed, and Tobias took another drink. "I think it's worth noting."

Deacon sat back down. "Okay. How about some dessert?"

Chapter Eighteen

"Hmm. Seems to be a Carmichael trait."

Riley was asleep when Gemma got home, so after she changed into her pajamas, she kissed him and tucked him in, then sat with Preston for a moment. He was on the small couch with a book.

He set his book down, then glanced at her. "So, how was it?"

"It was really nice. This is quite the family Cassidy has gotten involved with. She's very lucky."

"Hmm."

"What's that supposed to mean?"

Preston shrugged. "It's all so...pretentious. No one is this happy, or successful, or perfect. They have skeletons. You just haven't seen them yet."

"Sounds like someone is jealous."

"Of the Carmichaels? No way. I'll be glad to leave on Monday, though."

Gemma stood. "If you're so unhappy, you could leave in the morning. I don't want you to suffer through another day and a half with the Carmichaels."

He reached for her hand. "Calm down. That's not what I meant. I know you're having a good time with Cassidy. And...Tobias."

"He's very nice. Riley likes him. And he's fun to be around."

"Unlike me?"

"Actually, yeah."

"There are more important things to be than fun."

"Are there? I'm beginning to wonder." She pulled her hand away from him. "I'll see you in the morning."

"Gemma?"

She kept walking and went into her room and closed the door between the two. "Possibly the most un-fun person in the universe."

She realized she was thirsty, so she put a sweater on over her pajamas and opened the bedroom door. The house was dark except for a light coming from the partially closed door to the den. When she heard someone playing the piano, she moved to the door and looked through the opening. Tobias was sitting at the piano, quietly playing. She was astounded. He was really good.

She stepped into the room. "Tobias?"

He stopped playing and turned to look at her. "Hey there."

She crossed the room to him. "You play the piano?"

"It would seem so. Eight years of piano lessons. My mother thought it might have a calming effect on me." He shrugged. "She was wrong."

"You're full of surprises. What other hidden talents do you have?"

"Not drawing nudes."

"I think we established that already."

He lifted his leg over the piano bench and straddled it. "I play a fair game of chess. I'm not bad at poker. You've seen me play pool. And I make a hell of a ham sandwich. Are you hungry?"

"Not really."

"Do you want to watch me eat a ham sandwich?"

"Sure. Is that one of your talents, too?"

He laughed. "No. But I'm pretty good at it."

He stood, and as they left the room, Gemma took his arm when he turned off the light.

"I guess I should've left that on."

They made their way to the kitchen, and he turned on the light. "There we go. Made it." He went to the refrigerator and took out what he needed for his sandwich. "When Tanner was a kid, he had these little cars. Not Hot Wheels. They were tiny, like an inch long. He must have had fifty of them. And at any one time, a third of them would be on the floor, lying in wait for someone to step on them." He glanced at her. "I guess you know how that is. Boys and their toys."

"Yeah. I do."

"You sure you don't want a sandwich? I can make you a half." She shook her head, and he held up a piece of cheese. "Provolone?"

She took the cheese from him. "Fine."

He built a sandwich with a lot of ham, cheese, lettuce, and tomatoes. Then sat at the counter next to Gemma. "Do you want a bite?"

"No. I did come out here to get a drink, though."

Tobias took a bite, then stood and went to the refrigerator. "Water, orange juice, iced tea." He held up a bottle with no label. "Whatever this is?"

"Water is fine." She tore off a piece of cheese and ate it.

He poured her some water, then returned to his seat. She watched him eat for a minute.

"You ate a giant steak for dinner, not three hours ago."

He shrugged. "Three hours is a long time between meals."

"Not for most people."

He took another bite and chewed it thoughtfully. "So you've been made an honorary member of the Carmichael family."

"Yes. That was very nice. But I wanted to ask you about what you said."

"About loving my brother?"

"No. It's obvious you do. I mean about what you said when Deacon told you he wanted you to take on some more responsibility on the business side of things."

"Oh, yeah. I'll do what I need to do." He took another bite of his sandwich.

She ripped off another piece of cheese. "You used the M word."

Tobias thought for a moment. "Mmm. I was a few rums in. I don't remember."

"Marriage. You said if I'd only stay here and marry you..."

"Oh, yeah. That M word."

"You were just kidding, right?"

He set his sandwich down and looked at her. "No. But if you're opposed to marriage, I'm fine shacking up with you, too. Do they call it that anymore?"

"Not in polite company." She looked at him for a moment. How could he be so sure of how he feels? "We barely know each other, Tobias."

"That's not true. I feel I know you more than anyone I've ever met."

"So, if I showed up on your doorstep, you'd expect me to move right in with you?"

He turned in his seat and took her hand. "First off, if you showed up at my doorstep, I'd be the happiest man in the world and I wouldn't care what happened after that. I know you have Riley to think about. And if you needed your own place, I'd understand. And if you have a problem with marriage, like I said. I'm fine either way."

She shook her head. "Tobias. I've never met anyone like you."

"And you never will again. I want to be honest with you. If you said let's get married tomorrow after Deacon and Cassidy, I'd say, hell yeah. On the other hand if you said you never wanted to get married, that'd be fine, too. I just want to be with you. I don't care about putting a label on the situation."

Here was this perfect man sitting in front of her. Someone who wanted to be with her. He didn't care about any of the stupid stuff people worry about. He'd be fine, living here with her and never venturing further than the gate on the highway. "Why didn't I meet you seven years ago? Why weren't you Riley's father instead of the asshole that doesn't want anything to do with him?"

"Were you married to him?"

"No. I didn't even like him that much. He was older. And I found out after the fact, married. So, I guess your first impression of me when I turned up here with Preston was more accurate than I'd like it to be."

"Never. I was wrong. I was shocked to see you and angry. Confused. Hurt, I guess. You had every right to slap me."

"No, I shouldn't have slapped you."

He rubbed his cheek as though he could still feel the sting of it. "Believe it or not. You're the first woman who's ever slapped me."

"That's not an honor I want to have. I'm really sorry."

"You can spend the rest of our lives making it up to me."

"You have to stop saying things like that."

"Okay. I'm sorry. I'll stop. Just so you know, even though I'm not saying it, I'm thinking it."

"Fair enough."

When Tobias frowned at something behind her, Gemma turned to see Preston in the kitchen entrance.

"Um...Riley woke up. He's asking for you."

"Oh. Okay." She turned back to Tobias. "I'll see you tomorrow."

"Sleep well, Gemma."

When she walked by Preston, he gave her a small smile. "I'll be there in a minute."

She glanced at Tobias, then left the kitchen.

"Did I interrupt something?"

"Nope. Just having a sandwich."

"I know you're interested in Gemma. I mean, it's pretty damn obvious."

"What's it to you, Preston? You and she aren't together."

"Still. We came together."

"Nothing is going on. I'm well aware Gemma is leaving the day after tomorrow. I have no intentions of interfering in her life. I know she has a job to go back to. Friends. Family. A life. I'm not an idiot."

"I don't want Gemma hurt. And there's Riley to think about."

"I'd never hurt either of them." Tobias looked at Preston. "Are we done here? I'd like to finish my sandwich in peace."

Preston sighed. "Sure. We're done."

Tobias watched him go, then picked up the remaining half of his sandwich. "Bastard."

He meant every word he said to Gemma. He'd marry her in a second if that's what she wanted. He knew in his soul they were meant to be together. And the only thing that'd get him through her leaving, is believing someday she'd be back. He finished his sandwich, then went to Gemma's door and knocked softly.

A moment later, she opened it. She'd taken off her sweater, and he smiled when he saw her t-shirt. "Metallica?"

She shrugged. "It was a phase."

"I hope you're past it."

"Definitely." She leaned on the door frame. "Why are you here?"

"I wanted to make sure Riley was okay."

"He's fine. He had a dream, and it woke him up, and then he wanted to be reassured I was home."

"I know the feeling. Family breakfast tomorrow. Then you girls are going to lock yourselves in Abby's room, I guess, to get all prettified."

"That's the plan. What will you, Deacon, and Tanner be doing?"

"Whatever Deacon wants to do. I'll be by his side. Unless he doesn't want me by his side. Then I'll just linger a safe distance away."

"Is he nervous?"

"As far as I can tell, not in the least. He knew from day one she was the one."

"Hmm. Seems to be a Carmichael trait."

He took a deep breath. "One more day. Let's make it a day to remember."

"I'd like that."

"Something to tell our grandchildren about."

She nudged him. "Stop."

He laughed. "Sorry. I couldn't resist."

She put a hand on his arm. "I don't want you to think I haven't thought about it. That I haven't been tempted to say screw Austin."

"I know. Because I know you."

She shook her head. "There's so much that you don't know."

"I know the important stuff." He leaned in close to her. "And I know just where to touch you to—"

She put a hand on his mouth. "Don't."

He took a step back. "Good night, Gemma."

She nodded, then closed the door.

Tobias stayed for a moment. This isn't what he wanted. But it was all he was going to get for now. He put a hand on the door, then turned and headed for the stairs.

Chapter Nineteen

"Don't get any ideas."

E veryone was at the table when Tobias came into the dining room.

"Sorry. I overslept." Ruthie came in and set a plate down hard in front of him. "Sorry, Ruthie."

He glanced at their mother's empty chair. "So, what are we men doing today? It'll take us about thirty minutes to get dressed for the wedding, so we have several hours to kill."

Deacon smiled. "I wouldn't mind taking a ride."

Cassidy put a hand on his arm. "A nice gentle ride. No galloping. Or jumping trees. I'd like the Carmichael men to be in one piece for the wedding."

"We'll take it easy."

Riley folded his arms across his chest. "What am I going to do today?"

Preston patted his arm. "I thought you and I could go into town and find something to do for a couple of hours."

Tobias grinned. "Hmm. Let's see, there's a miniature golf place. Sort of. It's kind of lame. And then there's..." He shook his head. "That's about it."

Abby scowled at Tobias, then smiled at Riley. "There's ice cream at the coffee shop. They have like twenty different toppings to choose from."

Riley grinned. "That. I want to do that."

Gemma nudged him. "Then eat that breakfast, mister." She looked at Abby. "So there's really not a lot to do in Connelly. What do you do on a date?"

"Well, there is a bowling alley. A movie theater. And there's a dance at the grange every Saturday night."

"A dance?"

"Yeah. Open to everyone. They can be fun. If you don't mind hanging out with everyone in town from newborn to eighty."

"Sounds interesting."

Deacon cleared his throat. "The lack of things to do is why the local kids end up getting into trouble. We're fortunate to have Briarwood right here in town. The after-school programs they offer, along with Abby and Tanner's interest in our local rodeo community, keep them busy and out of mischief."

"Would you have shipped us off to some boarding school if Briarwood wasn't here?"

"Yes, Abby. I would've sent you to boarding school and only let you come home for Christmas and summer break."

"I wouldn't doubt it."

Deacon shook his head. "I'm not the monster you think I am."

Abby smiled. "I know. I actually liked going to Briarwood for twelve years with the same kids. Same cliques. Same drama. Same boys."

Gemma smiled. "How did you end up with such a prestigious school in your tiny town?"

Abby glanced at Deacon. "The Texas Ten. What they want, they get."

Deacon smiled at Gemma. "It's centrally located."

Gemma looked at Tanner. "How about you? Do you like the school?"

"Sure. It lets me move at my own pace. I'll have earned my AA by the time I graduate next year."

"That's wonderful."

Cassidy smiled. "He's a smart one."

Tanner shrugged. "I don't know about smart. I just like to learn stuff. And it means I'll only have to be gone two years to get my degree."

"Gemma, we're surrounded by smart people." She nudged Deacon. "This one here graduated from Yale with a 4 point something he's yet to disclose to me."

"Wow." Gemma looked at Tobias. "How about you?"

"I'm the underachiever of the group."

Abby shook her head. "You weren't an underachiever. You just didn't want to be at Yale."

Deacon picked up his orange juice. "Ruthie? Do we have a bottle of champagne in the kitchen?"

She came into the dining room. "Of course. I'll be right back."

"We are going to toast my lovely soon to be wife, and not talk about GPAs or being somewhere we don't want to be. Is everybody okay with that?"

Everyone agreed as Ruthie returned with the champagne and six glasses, then handed it to Deacon. "Ruthie, grab yourself a glass and bring one for Tanner, too."

She rushed off and returned with two glasses and a third with something bubbly in it. "This is for the young man." She smiled at Gemma. "Grape juice and sparkling water."

"Thank you."

Deacon filled all the glasses, and Ruthie handed them out. Then he stood and raised his glass. "This is the first wedding in the Carmichael family in thirty-five years. Let's not wait another thirty-five for the next one. I'm counting on the three of you to join me soon." He looked at Abby and Tanner. "Not too soon, though." He smiled at Ruthie. "You're still young, Ruthie. Maybe you'll find a second love of your life."

She laughed. "One was quite enough. God rest his soul."

"Thank you all for being here to celebrate this day with Cassidy and me."

Tobias raised his glass. "Wouldn't miss it, brother."

They all drank to the toast and Deacon sat down. Cassidy put her arm around him and kissed him. "It really is today, isn't it?"

"Yep. Today's the day."

———————

After breakfast, the women went up to Abby's room and began the process of getting ready for the wedding. Deacon, Tobias, and Tanner headed for the barn. As they passed through the kitchen, Ruthie took Deacon's arm.

"Mrs. Carmichael is still not herself."

He sighed. "I know. I saw her this morning."

"What do you want me to do? I can't leave her alone and go to the wedding."

Deacon put his hands on her shoulders. "Ruthie. I need you to be there. Call Mrs. Griffith, she can come stay with Mother."

"Are you sure?"

"I'm sure."

She smiled. "I didn't want to miss it."

"And we don't want you to miss it. Winston's still in the hospital. Cassidy's parents refused to come. You're our de facto mother, Ruthie. You always have been."

She kissed him on the cheek. "It's been my pleasure to fill in when I was needed."

"You've done much more than fill in."

She stepped away from him and dabbed at her eyes with the corner of her apron. "I need to save my tears for the wedding."

As the men left the kitchen and walked across the yard to the barn, Tanner glanced at Deacon.

"I'm sorry Mother's not well enough to be there for you, Deacon."

Deacon patted his back. He was disappointed, but he was also relieved. With as unpredictable as their mother had been lately, there was no telling what might have happened.

"It was always questionable whether she'd make it or not."

"I guess. But still."

Tobias glanced back at them. "Where should we ride to? Angel Falls? I've still never been behind the waterfall."

Tanner looked at him. "Behind the waterfall?"

Deacon nodded. "Yeah. Let's go there. I'll show you my and Dad's favorite spot."

They saddled their horses, then headed across the field toward the waterfall on the edge of their property. The Verde River originated in Oklahoma before flowing through miles of Forest Service land. It then dropped over a fifty-foot cliff and formed a pool of crystal clear water on Starlight Ranch property.

The men had all grown up swimming there in the hot Texas summers. But only Deacon was aware of the secret passage on the left side of the falls that let you go in behind the water. It was a spot their father had shown Deacon when he was a child. Today seemed like a good day to share it with his brothers.

They made it to the falls in less than an hour and dismounted. Then they tied the horses to the oak trees surrounding the pond. It was too early in the year to swim, and the water was high from the winter runoff.

Tobias walked to the edge of the water and put his hand in it. "Shit. That's cold."

Deacon headed for the path. "Come on."

Tanner and Tobias followed Deacon up the path, which ended a few feet into the heavy brush. They climbed over a series of boulders and came out on top of one about twenty feet below the top of the falls.

"Here we are." Deacon squeezed between the trunk of a twisted oak and a boulder and his brothers followed him. They came out onto a ledge protruding behind the flow of water.

Tanner grinned. "Whoa. This is so cool."

Tobias nodded and looked down at the pool below them. "Did you ever jump off?"

Deacon shook his head. "No. Don't get any ideas."

"It's not that far."

"It's at least thirty feet. And there are rocks down there."

"Not under the falls. They're by the edge and on the right side. Below the falls is the deepest part of the pool."

"Tobias. No. We promised not to be reckless."

"No, you promised not to be reckless." He nudged Tanner. "What do you say, kid?"

Tanner looked over the edge. "Nah. I don't think so. Deacon's right. It's pretty far."

"Tell you what. I'll go first. If I survive. You jump, too."

Deacon raised a hand. "Don't be talking sensible Tanner into doing something stupid."

"Fine." Tobias glanced at Tanner. "You don't have to go. But I'm doing it." He grinned at Deacon. "It'll be fine."

"Just so you know. I'm not jumping in after you when you don't come up."

Tobias slapped Deacon's shoulder. "Sure you will." He took off his shirt and his boots, then took off his pants. He handed everything to Tanner. "See you on the other side."

Deacon scowled. "Tobias, I swear, if you get hurt, I'll never forgive you."

Tobias covered his privates with his hands, then leaped off the ledge.

Deacon said, "Shit." He headed to the path to make sure Tobias made it.

Tanner followed him and they found Tobias swimming for the edge of the pond.

"Dammit, Tobias."

He climbed out of the water. "Now that was fun." He hugged his body and shivered. "And really, really cold."

"I hope you catch pneumonia."

Tanner handed Tobias his clothes. "You're crazy."

"You got to be a little crazy every once in a while just to know you're alive."

Deacon sat on a rock and watched Tobias sit on another with a grimace. "You hurt yourself."

"No. I'm good." He rubbed his thigh. "A little awkward tweak. I'll be good as new in a few minutes."

Deacon gave him thirty minutes to dry off in the sun, then Tobias got dressed. When Tobias mounted his horse, Deacon knew he wasn't over it. His brother had always been a little unpredictable and took chances he shouldn't. But it seemed ever since he got hurt, he'd been more reckless, as though he had to prove to himself he wasn't limited in what he could do. Deacon usually put up with it. But today was his wedding day, and Tobias should've been more careful.

Deacon was quiet on the ride back, and when they could see the ranch buildings, Tobias came up beside him.

"I'm sorry."

Deacon glanced at him, but didn't respond.

"Seriously, man, I was an idiot. But I'm fine. Nothing is going to keep me from standing next to you today."

Deacon nodded. "You can be an idiot all you want, but not on my wedding day, and don't try to talk Tanner into being one, too."

"Got it."

As they pulled up to the barn, Tobias wasn't sure if he'd be able to get off of Chance without help. His leg was on fire. But he didn't want

Deacon to know how much pain he was in. He sat for a moment, debating his options.

Deacon dismounted and handed his reins to Tanner. "Will you put him away for me?"

"Sure." Tanner glanced at Tobias, then took the two horses into the barn.

Deacon looked up at Tobias. "You need to get down sooner or later."

"Yeah. About that." He gave Deacon a little smile. "I might need some assistance."

Deacon shook his head. "I should make you get down by yourself. I should turn around and walk right to the house."

"But you won't. Because even though you hate me right now. You still love me."

Deacon smiled. "I really do hate you sometimes."

"I know. I hate me sometimes, too."

Deacon helped Tobias off of Chance, then gave him a minute to steady himself. "Can you stand?"

Tobias tried putting weight on his leg and swore. "Nope. Not happening."

Deacon put an arm around him and helped him to a pickup. He dropped the tailgate, before sitting Tobias down on it. "I'll go get Gemma."

"No. I'll be fine."

"You can't stand up. How is that being fine? The wedding is in two hours."

"Right. Go get Gemma."

Tanner came out of the barn. "What's going on?"

"Your idiot brother messed up his damn leg."

"Shit."

"Stay here with him. Don't let him move."

"Where are you going?"

"To get Gemma, who I hope can perform a miracle on my best man."

Chapter Twenty

"I'm not a magician."

When someone knocked on Abby's bedroom door, Gemma went to it.

"Who is it?"

"It's me, Ruthie."

Gemma opened the door. "Would you like to come in and see our beautiful bride?"

"I'd love to. But I'm here for Deacon. He needs to speak to you."

"Me?" She glanced at Cassidy, who left the mirror and came to the door.

"What's going on?"

Ruthie stepped into the room and smiled at Cassidy. "Don't you look beautiful." She patted her arm. "It's nothing for you to worry about."

"Which means I need to worry. Ruthie, what's going on?"

"It's Tobias. He's in a bit of pain and—"

"What happened?"

"Really, Miss Cassidy, I don't know. Deacon said to get Miss Gemma and not to upset you."

"Too late."

Gemma took Cassidy's hand. "I'm sure it's nothing. I'll go see what he needs."

"Thank you."

Gemma's hair and makeup were done, but she was still in jeans and a t-shirt. She slipped on some shoes and picked up her phone. "I'll call you with an update."

She left the room and followed Ruthie down the stairs.

"Where is he?"

They entered the kitchen, where Deacon was waiting. "Is she freaking out?"

"A little bit, yeah. What's going on?"

"Tobias. Tobias is being Tobias."

Gemma followed him out the door. "What's that mean?"

"He hurt his leg doing something stupid."

They crossed the grass to the barn and came up to Tobias, who smiled when he saw her. "Whoa. Look at you."

"What did you do?"

He shrugged. "Jumped off Angel Falls."

"You did what?"

"Not from the top. From about thirty feet. Jumping from the top would be really stupid."

Gemma looked at Deacon. "Call Cassidy and tell her everything is going to be fine. I really don't want to be the one to lie to her."

Deacon nodded, then scowled at Tobias. "I'm going to call my soon-to-be wife and lie to her."

"Sorry. But it's going to be fine."

Deacon took his phone out of his pocket and walked off.

Gemma looked at Tobias. "What possessed you to make a thirty foot jump three hours before you had to stand up for your brother?"

He grinned at her. "You really look beautiful."

"Tobias."

"Sorry. I wasn't thinking. Besides, it was water."

"Which becomes quite hard when you enter it from thirty feet up."

"Yeah. I found that out. It was like hitting a wall."

She put her hand on his knee. "How bad is it?"

"Um...on a scale of one to ten, about...thirty-seven."

She put her hands on her hips. "Can you stand on it?"

"Nope."

"Do you have crutches?"

"No. I burned them. But I wouldn't use them, anyway. I need to stand on my own two feet. No crutches. No cane."

"You should've thought about that before you jumped off the waterfall."

He pointed at her. "You need to fix it."

She laughed. "I'm not a magician."

"I don't want to be drunk. So rum is out."

"You think?" She put her hands on his thigh and felt around.

Tobias winced. "You need to numb it."

"With?"

"I don't know. You're the physical therapist."

"I'm here on vacation. I don't have my physical therapist tool kit with me."

Tobias thought for a moment, then looked at Tanner. "You're the horse guy. What do we use when a horse is hurt to numb their pain?"

"Analgesic liniment." He grinned. "But if it's really bad, we just shoot them."

Gemma shook her head. "You've been spending too much time with your brother. Horse liniment isn't safe for humans."

Tobias took another moment. "What about that cold stuff?"

"Biofreeze?"

"Yeah. That stuff."

"I don't know, man."

Tobias waved toward the barn. "Go get it. Let's read the label."

Tanner looked at Gemma.

She shrugged. "Let's see what it says."

Tanner headed for the barn, and Tobias smiled at Gemma. "Sorry to interrupt you and the ladies." He studied her for a moment. "Your hair is... In the sun..."

Gemma had never had anyone look at her the way Tobias looked at her. And it momentarily made her forget that he'd just jumped off a thirty-foot cliff.

Tanner came back with a bottle in his hand, and handed it to Gemma. She took a moment to read the label. "So, this is actually made for humans. You use it on your horses?"

"Yeah. Dr. Benton gave it to us."

"Okay."

Tobias tried to get comfortable, but didn't seem to have much luck. "So, it'll work?"

Gemma returned to him. "It will help a little. But if you actually damaged your leg further, then don't expect a miracle."

"I just need to walk." He smiled. "And maybe get in a dance or two."

She sighed. "Okay. Drop your pants."

Tobias grinned. "Here you are trying to get my pants off again."

Tanner blushed. "I ah...I'll be in the barn."

Gemma looked at him. "No you don't. I need you to stay here to make sure Tobias behaves himself."

It looked like it was the last thing Tanner wanted to do, but he said, "Yes, ma'am."

Tobias slid down to the ground and put his weight all on his right leg. He then unzipped his pants and let them drop to his boots. He glanced at Gemma before sitting back down.

She went to him. "Tanner, can you get me some latex gloves please?"

"Sure." He jogged off to the barn.

Gemma felt around Tobias' thigh. "You're muscles are a mess again. I'm going to put some of this on, then massage it in. It might get you to the altar. You better bring it with you, though. I'm not sure how long it'll last."

"Will you keep it for me? It won't fit in my suit pocket. And I'm leaving my purse behind."

"I'll bring it."

Tanner returned with a pair of gloves for Gemma and she put them on. "Okay, Tanner, I think you can go now. You should probably start getting ready."

"Right." He seemed relieved to leave the situation behind as he jogged for the house.

Gemma opened the bottle of gel and started massaging it in. She could tell it hurt Tobias, but he was trying not to show it. When it started to work, she could feel him relax a little.

"Is it working?"

"Yeah. I think so. It's kind of like shooting me full of ice water. It's an interesting sensation. Why didn't someone tell me about this stuff a long time ago?"

"It's a temporary fix, Tobias. If you want long-term relief, you need to do what we talked about."

"A program."

"Yes."

"You send it. I'll follow it."

She studied him for a moment. "Do you promise?"

"Scout's honor."

She raised an eyebrow. "Were you a boy scout?"

"Nope. Deacon was, though."

"Yeah. I can see that."

Tobias laughed. "It's kind of obvious."

Gemma smiled, then stopped when she saw Preston approaching. He stopped walking when he saw Tobias with his pants around his ankles.

Tobias grinned. "Hey, Preston."

"What the hell is going on?"

Gemma stepped away from Tobias. "He hurt his leg. Or re-hurt it...I was just—What are you doing here? Where's Riley?"

"I sent him in to get cleaned up."

"He's six. He needs help."

"I know. I was just curious as to what you were doing over here, since you should be getting ready yourself."

"Tobias needed help."

"No one else could rub medicine into his leg? Or maybe he could do it himself?"

She glared at Preston. "First off, it's none of your business what I do to Tobias." She took a moment. "Let me rephrase that."

"Don't bother. I think I get it." Preston turned. "I'll go help your son get ready."

Gemma watched him go, then looked at Tobias who was smiling at her.

"What?"

"You're really cute when you're flustered."

"I wasn't flustered. I was frustrated."

"Okay."

She smiled, then laughed. "The look on his face." She took off the gloves. "Put your pants back on, please."

"Are you sure?"

"Absolutely."

He slid off the tailgate again and tested his leg. "I can almost walk." He pulled his pants up and fastened them, then sat down again.

"Do you need help getting to the house?"

"I don't want to mess you up. I'm slightly damp."

"Do you have the keys to the truck?"

"They're in the ignition."

"I'll drive you to the porch."

Tobias managed to get himself upstairs and into his room, and Deacon showed up a few minutes later. He was in a charcoal suit with a black shirt and lighter gray tie. Tobias was tucking his gray shirt into charcoal pants.

Deacon looked at him for a long moment. "Did she fix you?"

"Temporarily." He patted his leg. "Good as new."

"Somehow, I don't quite believe that."

Tobias picked up his black tie and went to the bathroom mirror. He came out a few moments later with it tied. His leg still hurt quite a bit, but he could put weight on it. He tried not to limp as he went to his jacket hanging on the back of a chair. He slipped it on, then smiled at Deacon.

"We look pretty damn good."

Tanner came through the door. "Hey. Damn tie."

Deacon waved him over. "I'll do it."

Tanner was dressed like Tobias, and the three of them together were quite impressive. Tanner was shorter than his older brothers. He was five-ten, compared to Deacon's six-one, and Tobias at six-two.

Tobias patted Tanner's shoulder. "You are our little brother in more ways than one."

"Shut up."

Tobias pulled him in and kissed him on the cheek. "I'm just kidding. Someone had to inherit the blond, blue-eyed, short in stature, genes from Mother's side of the family."

Tanner pulled away from him and wiped his cheek. "Well, I've heard women like guys with blue eyes."

Tobias nodded. "It's true. They do."

Tanner eyed him. "And...?"

"Nothing. That's it. You're a handsome kid. I'll admit it."

Deacon headed for the door. "We're leaving in five. Cassidy wants us out of the house when they emerge from Abby's room."

"We're coming."

As Tobias and Tanner got to the stairs, Tobias took Tanner's arm. "Help your tall, dark-haired, gray-eyed brother down the stairs."

Tanner put his arm around Tobias' waist. "I almost wish I'd taken the jump."

Tobias leaned on Tanner as they went down the stairs. "Kid, you're a lot smarter than I am."

"Still."

"Save it for summer. At least you won't freeze your ass off."

Tanner laughed. "That's the least of it, isn't it?"

Tobias nodded. "Yeah. I guess you're right."

Deacon was at the bottom of the stairs. "Come on. Let's go."

Tobias smiled at him. "Calm down. Relax. Take a breath."

"I'm plenty calm."

"No. You're not. You're wired. Come on."

"Where?"

"To the den. We need to have a drink before we go."

Deacon took a deep breath. "Okay. One drink."

"One drink."

They entered the den, and Tobias went behind the bar and poured three shots of scotch. He handed a glass to Deacon and Tanner, then held up the third one.

"To the Carmichael brothers. Family. Honor. Loyalty."

Tanner nodded. "And horses."

Deacon laughed. "And good women."

Tobias tapped their glasses. "And good scotch."

Chapter Twenty-One

"You know me. Sweet Tobias."

T he Carmichael brothers went into the secret garden area. It was a circular space edged by twenty-foot Italian Cypress. The ground was covered with bricks laid down a century ago, and had moss growing in the cracks between them.

There were two sections of chairs, divided by a walkway ending at the small altar. The area had been decorated with twinkle lights in the trees, pots of flowers on the benches around the edges of the space, and two dozen candles on the altar. There was a piano with a music stand next to it for the violinist.

It was breathtaking, and Deacon stopped at the entrance for a moment to take it all in.

Tobias put a hand on his back. "Wow. This is incredible."

Deacon nodded and took a breath. "Yeah. It sure is."

Pastor Joe walked down the aisle to meet them. He shook Deacon's hand. "How you doing, son?"

"Good. I'm good."

"We have about a half-hour until showtime. Folks should start arriving soon. You boys can sit or stand to the side. Whatever you want to do."

Deacon looked at Tobias. "You should sit."

He nodded. "Yeah. I'll take a load off for a minute."

A few minutes later, the pianist and violinist came in and once they got set up, they began playing. Shortly after that, the guests started arriving.

Tanner smiled at Deacon. "I guess I should go find the women. I'm supposed to walk with Abby." He shook Deacon's hand. "I'm happy for you, man."

Deacon pulled him in for a hug. "I'll see you soon."

As more people started arriving, Tobias got up and the two of them stood off to the side.

He grinned at Deacon. "You got this."

"I know. I'm fine."

"I never thought this day would come. Up until six months ago, anyway."

Deacon nodded. "I'm as surprised as you are. But it's good. And it's right. And I couldn't be happier."

"I know." He patted Deacon's chest. "You deserve this, man. You've been taking care of everyone else for far too long."

"Well, that's not going to change."

"Maybe not. But it's a lot easier to put in the day's work when you have someone to go home to. Or at least that's what I've heard. I wouldn't know from personal experience."

"You'll get your day, Tobias."

"I'm not so sure about that."

"I am."

Cassidy had picked a simple, yet very elegant, wedding dress. The full skirt was cocktail length and made with multiple layers of fine tulle. The satin bodice was strapless, and she wore a lace bolero length jacket with three sets of ribbons tied in tiny bows keeping it closed. Her veil was short and matched the skirt. It was secured to her hair with a headband of tiny white flowers.

Gemma gave her a hug. "You are the most beautiful bride."

"Thank you. I'm feeling quite beautiful." She looked at Abby. "Will he like it?"

Abby nodded. "Definitely."

Gemma's and Abby's dresses varied slightly, but both were a light mint green. They were knee length and Gemma's was silky and form fitting, and she loved it. Abby looked at her.

"Pretty sure Tobias is going to be rather fond of your dress as well."

Gemma smiled. "Is Skyler coming?"

"Yes."

"Well, then I think there will be three happy men at the reception."

Abby nodded. "We are pretty fierce."

Cassidy took both of their hands. "Thank you for being here for me on this wonderful day."

Gemma hugged her. "There's nowhere I'd rather be." She stood back and pointed at Cassidy. "No tears."

When someone knocked on the door, Gemma went to answer it. She was expecting it to be Tanner. But it was Tobias.

The sight of the six-foot-plus gorgeous cowboy standing at the door took her breath away. She took him in from his black boots to the gray hat on his head.

"What are you doing here?"

He took a step back. "First off, whoa!" He took a breath. "You are a vision."

She smiled. "You're not so bad yourself, Mr. Guy. But why are you here? Shouldn't you be standing next to your brother?"

Tobias smiled. "I have no idea why I'm here. It's completely flown out of my head."

She cocked her head. "Try to remember."

"Right. Deacon didn't want Cassidy to walk down the aisle by herself. So, if she's willing, I'd like to offer her my arm to escort her to the altar."

"That is—"

"So unbelievably sweet." Cassidy stepped up beside Gemma.

Tobias was again stunned. "Holy shit. Wow."

Cassidy smiled. "Um...thank you?"

"You just may get a kiss from Deacon to rival the carnal classroom kiss."

Gemma laughed. "What's this now?"

Tobias winked at her. "I'll explain later."

Abby came to the door, and Tobias glanced at her. "Oh, hey, sis."

Abby punched him in the shoulder. "Hey, sis?"

He laughed. "I'm joking. You're beautiful, Abigale."

"Thank you. As are you."

Tanner came up behind Tobias. "I think it's time. Does anyone want to admire me? Tobias and I are wearing the same thing."

Abby hugged him. "A dashing cowboy." She adjusted his hat.

He readjusted it. "Thanks."

Tobias rubbed his hands together. "So, are we ready?"

Cassidy nodded. "I'm very ready."

"Then let's go get you married."

⸻

They left the Connelly house and walked through the flower gardens toward the circle of Italian Cypress.

Tobias leaned in to Cassidy's ear. "You know. It's not too late to change your mind. I could nudge Deacon aside and you could marry me instead."

"Tempting. But I think I'll stick with the original plan."

"Okay. Just thought I'd give it a shot."

"Besides, I'm pretty sure there's someone else here who you'd much rather spend your life with."

"Hmm. I have no idea what you're talking about."

They reached the entrance and stopped while Tanner and Abby went through it, followed by Gemma.

Tobias patted Cassidy's hand. "You all good?" She took a breath, then nodded, and they went through the entrance. He felt her hesitate when she caught sight of Deacon, and Tobias could tell his brother was equally taken aback at the sight of his bride.

They continued down the aisle, then Tobias handed Cassidy over to Deacon and he took his place next to Tanner.

The ceremony was short and to the point, with Deacon and Cassidy exchanging vows they wrote. When they were pronounced husband and wife, Deacon took off his hat and handed it to Tobias, then took Cassidy in his arms and kissed her.

Tobias and Tanner both whistled while the guests got to their feet and clapped. Deacon retrieved his hat, before he and Cassidy walked down the aisle. Tobias took Gemma's hand and followed them, with Tanner and Abby bringing up the rear.

They spent the next twenty minutes in the flower garden greeting the guests. When Tobias noticed Gemma had wandered off, he went looking for her. He found her back in the secret garden.

"Hey. What are you doing in here?" She turned to him with tears in her eyes, and he took a step back. "Why are you crying?"

She shook her head. "I have no idea." She wiped her eyes. "Now I'm going to be a mess."

He stepped up to her and wiped away a couple of her tears. "No harm done."

She looked at him for a moment. "I'm just really happy for Cassidy. She's so lucky to have found not only Deacon, but all of you."

"We're the lucky ones to have her."

"I feel so bad that her stupid parents couldn't put their feud aside and come to their daughter's wedding. And then Winston got sick. And your mother."

"Hey. It's all good. She and Deacon have made their peace with that."

Gemma nodded. "I suppose. It was very sweet of you to walk her down the aisle."

He shrugged. "You know me. Sweet Tobias."

"Can I ask sweet Tobias a favor?"

"Anything."

"Will you...kiss me?"

He grinned. "Of course. And I hate myself for asking this, but why?"

"I just need to have a little bit of Malady Springs back."

Tobias put his hands on her face, then kissed her. He smiled, then kissed her again.

Gemma put her hands over his and then stepped back. "That's enough. It's as good as I remembered." She held his gaze for a moment, then looked away. "We should get back. It's about time for pictures."

"Yay, my favorite."

"You don't like your picture taken?"

He shrugged. "I don't mind."

"How's your leg?"

"I'm still standing."

The photo session lasted an hour, and when Tobias and Gemma entered the flower gardens where the reception was being held, she spotted Preston and Riley.

"I should go sit with them." She looked at him. "You're welcome to come."

"No thanks. I'm not going to spend the evening with Preston. But I understand why you need to. I'm about ready for a drink."

They parted ways, and Tobias headed for the bar set up on one side of the garden space. He sat on one of six stools, which were currently all empty.

He smiled at the female bartender. "I'll take a rum, straight up, please."

She nodded and poured a healthy shot into a glass, then set it in front of him. "Don't tell me the best man is flying solo tonight."

He picked up his glass. "Afraid so." He ignored the invitation in her eyes and took a sip of rum. Another guest came to the bar, and she went to help them.

He turned his back to the bar, as he mumbled, "Another day, another time, lady." He only had eyes and a heart for Gemma, who was currently laughing it up with her ex-boyfriend. When Abby and Skyler came up to him, he smiled at them.

"Abigale. Fremont."

Skyler looked good, as he always did. And Tobias still couldn't understand why Abby insisted they were just friends. He was pretty sure Skyler was willing to leave the friend zone behind.

"Did your old man come?"

Skyler shook his head. "He's conveniently out of town. But he sent a very expensive gift to make up for his absence."

"I'm sure he did."

"Abby told me about your mother. I'm sorry, man."

Tobias sighed. "Yeah. I guess the whole town will finally know she's not the woman she's been pretending to be the last few years."

"It's nobody's damn business. They won't hear anything from me."

"I know. I'm only going to admit this one time. You're a good man, Skyler."

Skyler grinned. "As are you, Tobias." He glanced at Abby. "For a Yale man."

Tobias laughed. "You had to go there."

Abby patted Tobias' knee. "I want a dance later. If you're up to it."

"Anytime."

"And please, take it easy on the rum."

Tobias looked at his glass. "Yes, ma'am."

Tobias ordered one more rum, then smiled when he saw Riley headed his way.

"Hey, little man, can I buy you a drink?"

Riley laughed. "I'm just a kid."

Tobias lifted him onto the stool next to him, then waved at the bartender. "Can you fix this gentleman a Roy Rogers please? Two cherries."

"Coming right up."

"What's a Roy Rogers?"

"Trust me. You're going to love it."

The bartender set the Coke and grenadine mix with two cherries floating on top, in front of Riley. The boy laughed. "Cool!"

Tobias tapped Riley's glass. "*Slàinte Mhath!*"

"What's that mean?"

"It's a cheer to your good health in Gaelic. The language of my ancestors."

"Cool." He took a sip of his drink, then dug out a cherry and ate it.

Tobias nudged him. "So, I saw you talking to that blonde a while ago."

Riley giggled. "Her name's Britney."

"Of course it is. Are you going to ask her to dance?"

Riley glanced toward the girl, who was a couple years younger than him. "Nah. She's just a baby."

"You like them a little older?"

Riley ate the second cherry. "Yeah. At least six,"

"Gotcha."

Chapter Twenty-Two

"You need to pace yourself."

Preston had found someone to talk to and Riley had wandered off to play with some kids, so Gemma went to visit with Cassidy, who was currently alone at a table.

She sat down. "Don't tell me Deacon left you alone."

"He's making the rounds. He knows everyone. I know about half of them." She glanced at Gemma. "I'm actually enjoying watching what's happening at the bar.

Gemma looked to see what Cassidy was talking about. Tobias and Riley were sitting at the bar, deep in conversation.

"Oh, my gosh. I can't even... Look at them."

Cassidy took her hand. "What are you going to do about this, Gem? I know you care for him as much as he cares for you."

Gemma sighed. "I don't know. Of course, I want to say the hell with everything and never leave."

"So, why don't you?"

She shook her head. "It's not that easy. I have a job I love. Friends. Family." She looked at Cassidy. "You had already made the move here when you met Deacon. You'd left Austin behind. You landed a great job here at the school. I ran into Tobias in a bar."

"I understand. It's a lot to consider. And a lot to give up."

"Am I being stupid? Am I being selfish?"

"You're doing what you need to do. And Tobias realizes that. When you get home and settle back into your life, you'll either know it's where you're supposed to be. Or—"

"I'll hate myself for leaving Tobias."

"Tobias will be here." She motioned toward the bar. "Go have a drink with those two handsome men."

Gemma nodded, then got to her feet. She crossed the garden and sat next to Tobias.

He smiled at her. "Hey there, Ms. Girl. Can I buy you a drink? Or do you want to get your own?"

"I believe the drinks are free."

He waved at the bartender. "A rum and Coke for the lady, please. And I'll have one more."

Gemma looked around Tobias at Riley. "What are you drinking, kiddo?"

"A Roy Rogers. It's really good."

"Sounds yummy."

He slurped the last of his drink. "Can I have another one?"

"Mmm. Let's wait. You can have another in a while."

Tobias patted Riley's shoulder. "You need to pace yourself."

Riley shrugged. "Okay." He slid off the stool. "Can I go play with my friends?"

Gemma smiled. "You made friends?"

"Yeah. Those kids over there."

"Sure, honey. Just don't leave the garden." Riley ran off and Gemma looked at Tobias. "What were you two talking about?"

"Guy stuff. Girls, sports, stuff like that."

"I see. And what did my six-year-old son have to say about girls?"

"He likes them to be at least six."

"That sounds reasonable. How about you? How old do you like your girls?"

He looked at her for a moment. "How old are you?"

"Twenty-seven."

"When's your birthday?"

"January twenty-first."

"I guess I like my girls a couple of months older than me, then." He put a hand on his chest. "March thirtieth."

"So you recently had a birthday."

"Yes, I did."

"And how do the Carmichaels celebrate birthdays?"

"Cake, candles, lots of presents."

"Really?"

"Nah. We have cake with a candle or two. And modest gift giving. They all got me a new saddle."

"That's not that modest."

"Yeah. It's not a Ferrari though."

She studied him for a moment. "You really don't look like the Ferrari type."

"Only if they made a truck."

She took a sip of her drink. "I don't suppose you'd dance with me?"

He finished off his rum. "I'd love to."

They went to the dance floor and Tobias took Gemma in his arms. He was being a little formal, and he wouldn't meet her eyes when she looked at him.

"Tobias?"

"Yep."

"What's wrong?"

"I'm pretty sure you already know the answer to that question."

"I'm sorry."

He stopped dancing and looked at her. "Quit telling me you're sorry. It doesn't make me feel any better."

She glanced at the people around them and lowered her voice. "What do you want me to say?"

He shook his head. "Nothing. There's nothing to say." He tipped his hat, then turned and walked away from her.

Tobias was sitting at the piano in the secret garden when Gemma found him. She'd given him some time to cool down, which he appreciated. She sat down next to him, with her back to the piano.

"Are you hiding out?"

He finished the song he was playing. "Just getting some fresh air away from the celebration."

"Hmm. I'm pretty sure you're hiding out."

"Maybe a little." He reached for her hand. "Do you think if I don't go to bed tonight, tomorrow will never come?"

"I don't think it works like that." She laid her head on his shoulder.

He kissed her forehead and her cheek. Then he lifted her chin and kissed her on the lips. He whispered, "I don't want you to go."

"I know."

"Don't go."

She looked at him and they kissed again. He turned toward her and took her in his arms and kissed her like he had at the motel. She nuzzled his neck and kissed him back.

He spoke into her ear. "Come back to the house with me."

She nodded, and they got to their feet. He kissed her again, then she put her hands on his chest and stepped back. "I can't. Riley. I can't leave him here alone."

Tobias tried to catch his breath and slow his racing heart. He put his forehead against hers. "You're right. This isn't how we want it to be." She laid her head against his shoulder and he kissed her hair. "I can't watch you leave in the morning. This is our goodbye."

She nodded, then looked up at him and kissed him one more time. "Goodbye, Random Guy." He nodded and she left the garden.

Tobias sat on the bench and closed his eyes. When he heard someone behind him, he half-hoped it was Gemma when he glanced back. But it was Skyler.

He approached Tobias, picked up a chair, then sat it next to the piano bench and straddled it.

"Are you okay?"

"Do I look okay?"

"You look like your puppy got ran over by a car."

"Trust me. That wouldn't make me feel nearly as bad as I feel right now."

"Sorry, man."

Tobias looked at him. "Why are you here?"

"Deacon sent me to look for you. They're about to head out."

"Shit." Tobias got to his feet. "Don't want to miss that."

Skyler stood, and they left the garden. "I'm having trouble picturing Deacon in Hawaii."

"Yeah. You and me both. Talk about a fish out of water."

"Can you picture him in shorts and a Hawaiian shirt, sitting on the beach with a Mai Tai?"

Tobias smiled. "If that happens, Cassidy better get a picture of it."

Skyler put his hand on Tobias' shoulder. "If you ever need to talk, or just need someone to go have a beer with, I'm here."

Tobias nodded. "You're alright, for a Harvard man." They headed for the reception area. "So, what's with you and my sister?"

"That, I don't want to talk about."

"Come on. I get the feeling..."

Skyler shrugged. "I respect Abby. I like her...a lot. But it appears we're destined to be friends."

"Things often change."

"Yeah. Well, she's currently trying to find me a wife, so I'm not holding out much hope."

"The damn Carmichaels. We're never in the right place at the right time with the right person."

Skyler nodded toward Deacon and Cassidy, who were saying goodbye to everyone. "Well, at least one of you figured it out."

"Yep. Deacon always was the smart one."

While trying to avoid Gemma, Tobias hugged Cassidy and shook hands with Deacon.

"Enjoy yourself, and don't worry about anything here. I've got it."

Deacon didn't seem quite convinced. "Are you sure?"

"Yeah. I think I can keep things from imploding for two weeks."

Deacon smiled. "I believe you can." He put his arm around Cassidy and waved to the guests. "Thanks for coming, everyone."

They ran off to a waiting car and got inside. With one more wave, they were gone.

The medicine on his leg had long since worn off, and Tobias was in a lot of pain. He'd been trying to ignore it, but now he didn't want to anymore. He went to the bar and smiled at the bartender.

"Do you have a bottle of rum back there?" She held up one that was three-fourths full. He took it from her. "That should do it."

"Do you need a glass, cowboy?"

"No. That'll just slow me down."

He didn't have his own vehicle. They'd all come in the Escalade, so he got into the backseat, put his leg on the seat, and leaned against the door. He opened the bottle and took a sip. It wouldn't help the pain in his leg. But it might help him forget about Gemma for a few hours.

About half-way through the remaining rum, someone knocked on the window Tobias was leaning against. He moved away and squinted at Tanner as he opened the door.

"We've been looking all over for you."

"Well, you found me." Abby and Skyler came up behind Tanner. "Hey sis."

"Dammit, Tobias."

"I didn't know I had to check in with you before I checked out of the party." He took a drink from the bottle, then Skyler stepped up to the door and took it from him.

"That's probably enough."

Tobias scowled at him. "Are you my mother? Because I'm pretty sure she's still at home in la la land."

Abby shook her head. "Tobias, stop."

Skyler glanced at her, then looked back at Tobias. "We'll get you home."

"You'll get no argument from me. I wanted to go a half of bottle of rum ago."

Skyler turned to Abby. "Do you want me to follow you to the ranch?"

"No. Tanner and I can handle one drunk Carmichael."

He pointed at Tanner. "You drive. Abby has had a few glasses of champagne."

Tanner nodded and circled the vehicle to get behind the wheel. Tobias watched Abby say goodnight to Skyler. She gave him a hug, then kissed him on the cheek. He held onto her hand for a moment, before letting it go. Abby got into the front seat next to Tanner.

Tobias kicked her seat. "You know that guy's in love with you, right?"

She turned and looked at him. "Skyler?"

"Yeah. Hopelessly in love. I know what it looks like."

"We're just friends."

"No, *you're* just friends. Guys don't spend as much time with girls who want to be their friend as Skyler does with you."

Abby turned back around. "Even if that was true. I don't feel like that about him."

"Why not? He's good looking. Polite. He respects you. He follows you around like a puppy so he can step in and rescue you whenever necessary. And on top of that, he's loaded."

"Whatever. It's none of your business."

"Hey, Tanner. I'm right. Right?"

Tanner looked at him through the mirror. "I'm staying out of it."

"Coward."

Abby turned back around. "So, you and Deacon wouldn't have a problem with me falling for a Harvard man? And a Fremont?"

"I can accept the Harvard part. And as for being a Fremont? He's hardly his father's son."

Abby smiled. "That's the first thing you've said I agree with."

Chapter Twenty-Three

"Every woman wants a cowboy."

Gemma came off the porch with the last of her things. Abby and Tanner were at the car with Preston and Riley. Gemma put her stuff in the trunk.

"I guess that's it."

Preston closed the trunk, then shook hands with Tanner and Abby, before putting Riley in the backseat and getting in behind the wheel.

Gemma gave Tanner a hug. "It was really nice to meet you. Keep working on Deacon about the whole college thing. Maybe he'll cave."

"I doubt it. But I'll try."

When she hugged Abby, she said, "Take care of your older brother, will you?"

Abby took Gemma's hands. "I'm sorry he's not here. He took off on Chance a while ago. I'm not sure how, since he had quite a bit to drink last night after Deacon left."

"I figured he wouldn't be here. He said he wouldn't. We said goodbye last night. He probably shouldn't be on a horse, though, after yesterday."

"Well, that's my brother. Stubborn, irrational, and stupid."

Gemma smiled, "That pretty well describes him." She gave Abby and Tanner a small smile, looked around one last time, then got into the car. As Preston pulled away, she spotted a horse and rider coming fast across the field in the rearview mirror.

"Stop!"

"What?"

"Stop the car." Preston stepped on the brakes and Gemma opened her door and got out before it rolled to a stop. She moved away from the car as she watched Tobias gallop towards the ranch. When he got closer, he slowed a little, and she ran towards him. He pulled Chance to a stop and dismounted as Gemma got to him. He tossed his hat and threw his arms around her.

"I had to see you one more time."

They shared a kiss they'd both remember for a long time, then she smiled at him. "Thank you."

He put a hand on her cheek. "I'm an idiot. I shouldn't have said half the things I said to you."

"It's okay. I wanted to hear them."

He nodded and kissed her again. "You take care, Gemma."

"You too. It's been...surreal." She backed up a few steps, then turned and headed for the car. When she walked by his hat, she stopped and picked it up. She turned back. "I'm taking this with me."

He smiled. "It's my favorite hat."

"I know." She headed for the car again.

"I'm going to need that back at some point."

She stopped at the car and looked at him one more time, then got in.

Tobias watched the car until he couldn't see it anymore. Abby and Tanner walked to him and Abby put an arm around his waist.

He put his arm around her shoulders. "She took my damn hat."

"I have a really good feeling you're going to get it back."

"You do, huh?"

"Yep."

Tobias sighed. "What do you say, we go work with that damn stubborn Arabian?"

"We could sell him, you know."

"Never. That'd be giving in to him. I'm going to tame the bastard if it kills me."

Tanner laughed. "It just might. I keep telling you, you're doing it wrong."

Tobias looked at him. "How so?"

"You've got to communicate with him."

"I don't speak stubborn Arabian."

"Will you let me try?"

Tobias studied him for a moment. "Sure. Let's see what you've got."

The three of them headed for the barn. Before going in, Tobias glanced toward the road again, then followed Abby and Tanner inside.

Tanner put a line on Aladdin's halter and led him out of the barn and into the small training pen. He walked him around a few times, then stopped a few feet from the horse's head and looked at him.

"What's all this fuss, Aladdin? Don't you like Tobias? He doesn't get you, right?"

Tobias called from outside the pen where he and Abby were watching Tanner. "Right. It's my fault."

Tanner glanced at him, then returned his gaze to the horse. He walked closer and ran a hand down the horse's nose. Aladdin didn't back away, and kept eye contact with Tanner.

"There you go, boy. You just wanted someone to be nice to you. You don't like grumpy old Tobias."

Tobias shook his head. "Son of a bitch."

Abby nudge him. "Our brother, the horse whisperer."

Aladdin wasn't saddled, but Tanner looped the lead line around his neck and tied it to the other side of the halter. Then, after running his hands along Aladdin's side, he grabbed a handful of mane, and jumped onto his back. The horse remained calm and let Tanner get settled onto his back.

Tobias couldn't believe what he was seeing. "Are you kidding me?"

Tanner rode Aladdin around the pen with just a lead line and nothing else. He circled the pen several times at a walk, then urged the horse into a lope. After a few minutes, he stopped and slid off of Aladdin's back.

He smiled at Tobias. "And that's how it's done."

"You've just been promoted, kid. Training horses is now your full-time job. Until school starts, then it's your after school and on weekends job."

Tanner smiled. "I'll take it."

Abby went into the ring and patted Aladdin's nose. "I knew you were a sweetheart."

Tobias laughed. "No you didn't. I believe not thirty minutes ago, you were talking about selling the bastard."

She glanced at him. "Shush. Tanner just did in ten minutes what you couldn't do in seven months."

"I broke him in. Tanner came in during the fourth quarter and stole my thunder."

"Whatever."

Tobias waved a hand at them, then headed for the barn. He was actually really impressed. He'd seen Tanner with horses before and knew he had a gift, but that was pretty amazing. He unsaddled Chance and put him into his stall, then gave him a handful of oats.

"So, she's gone. I guess you know that. You were right there when she left. Had a front room seat to the kiss. I don't know if you could tell, being a horse and all, but it was a hell of a kiss."

Preston hadn't said anything about the kiss, which was fine with Cassidy. She didn't need any input from him. She watched the scenery go by and thought about Tobias while they drove in silence. Even Riley was quiet, lost in a game he was playing on his tablet.

She didn't understand how she could have fallen so hard, so fast, for someone so different from her. Different from anyone she'd ever known. When her phone buzzed with a notification, she pulled up her text messages. It was a picture from Cassidy of her and Deacon on the beach. Underneath the picture she wrote. *"We're here! Love you. Thank you so much for being there for me."* There were three heart emojis. Then she wrote, *"Every woman wants a cowboy. Don't let yours get away."*

Gemma smiled, then wrote back to her. *"He showed up this morning to say goodbye. I left with a kiss and his favorite cowboy hat."*

She answered. *"He's going to want that back."*

"I know."

Most of the trip was a blur. Preston continued to not say much and when she dropped him at his apartment eight hours later, he said goodbye to Riley and gave her a nod. She drove the four miles to her condo and she and Riley hauled their bags up the stairs to home.

She dropped hers by the door. "Take your stuff to your room. It's late. Brush teeth, go pee, and put on your pajamas. I'll be there in a few minutes to tuck you in."

She looked around the living room. She'd lived there for two years. It was the first place she was able to buy, and she'd been proud of herself for doing it. It was a big step toward adulthood. It was a mile from the clinic, and when the weather was good, she'd often ride her bike. They were right on the edge of the University grounds, and the streets were designed for bike and foot traffic. She'd built a good life for herself and Riley. And she was happy. At least she was when she left. Now she wasn't so sure.

She sat in a chair. It all seemed so small now. And the air seemed heavy with the smells of the city. As she was wondering what Tobias was doing, Riley called to her.

She stood. "I'm coming." She went in and sat on the edge of Riley's bed. "Well, we're home."

"Yeah."

"Just, yeah?"

He nodded. "I miss everything."

"The ranch?" He nodded. "And the horses?" He nodded again. "And...Tobias?"

He sat up and hugged her. "Especially Tobias."

"Me too, honey. Me too."

He pulled back and looked at her. "When can we go back?"

She smiled at him. "I don't know. We just got home. I have to go to work tomorrow. And you have three more weeks of school."

"Then summer!"

"Yes. Then summer. You have camp. And you get to spend time with Grandma and Grandpa."

"Can we go see Tobias this summer?"

She laid him down and tucked him in. "Tell me what you like about Tobias."

Riley smiled. "He's funny. And he's a cowboy."

"Yes. He's both of those things."

"But mostly, because he's my friend. He doesn't treat me like a kid."

Gemma nodded. "That's really important."

"It is."

"Okay. Bed."

"But you didn't answer my question."

"We'll talk about seeing Tobias again. But not tonight."

Riley sighed. "Okay. But don't forget."

"I won't." She kissed him, then left the room and turned off the light. "I love you, sweetheart."

"I love you, too, Mom."

Gemma turned off the lights in the living room, then went to her room and got ready for bed. When she laid down, she opened the photo gallery on her phone and looked at the pictures she'd taken the day of their trail ride. When she got to the one of Tobias and Riley sitting in the grass getting warm after their dunk in the creek, she stared at it for a long time.

"Tobias Carmichael. What is it about you?" She scrolled back to the ones Tobias had taken of him and Riley on the horse. "You silly, silly man. It seems my son has fallen for you, too."

Chapter Twenty-Four

"Some men are born to be cowboys."

S pending two weeks being Deacon wasn't fun, but it passed the time, and before he knew it, Tobias was waiting on the porch for Deacon and Cassidy to come home. They'd hired a car to bring them from the airport rather than have Tobias make the two-hour trip to pick them up.

When a car turned into the driveway, Abby went down the steps. Tanner and Tobias joined her as the car pulled in front of the house. Cassidy got out and greeted them while Deacon got their bags and tipped the driver. He walked over to them and set the bags down.

"Looks like everything's in order."

Tobias grinned. "I told you I could handle it." He shook Deacon's hand.

Abby took Cassidy's arm. "Ruthie made a beautiful lunch, and we want to hear all about your trip." They headed into the house.

Tobias put a hand on Deacon's shoulder. "Glad to be home?"

"You have no idea how much."

Tanner grinned. "You had enough of the ocean and the sand?"

Tobias added, "Hula dancers? Fruity drinks?"

"I'll tell you what I missed. Not sleeping in my own bed. The smell of coffee coming from the kitchen in the morning." He sniffed the air. "And the smell of green grass, Texas dust, and manure."

Tobias laughed. "Welcome home, brother."

They went inside and Deacon stopped in the middle of the living room and looked at Faith's door. "How is she?"

"Still waiting for Dad to come home."

"Has she asked where I was?"

"Whenever she did, I told her you were at school. She seemed to buy it."

"I should go see her."

Tobias put a hand on his shoulder. "Come eat first. Ruthie's excited to see you."

They ate a long and leisurely lunch while Cassidy told them all about Hawaii. Deacon interjected a few times, but mostly he let her tell it. It seemed they had a good time, despite it being so different from northern Texas. But Cassidy, like Deacon, was glad to be home.

They were finishing dessert when Deacon excused himself.

"I'm going to check in with Mother, then I'll be in the office."

Tobias nodded and watched him go, before smiling at Cassidy. "So, did you get him in a pair of shorts and flipflops?"

She laughed. "No."

"So, no swimming in the ocean?"

"Well, we did go swimming once."

"In jeans and cowboy boots?"

She shook her head. "No."

Tobias raised his hand. "Okay. I don't want to know anymore."

Abby giggled. "Go Deacon."

Tobias stood and picked up a few dirty dishes. "It's good to have you back, Cassidy."

"Thank you. It's really good to be home."

He took the dishes to the kitchen and set them on the counter next to the sink. Ruthie looked at him.

"Are you just carrying them in? Or are you volunteering to wash them, too?"

Before he could answer, he heard Deacon yell from his office. "Tobias!"

Tobias picked up a brownie and headed for the back door. "That's my cue to leave." He went through the door and headed for the barn. Deacon left a very organized desk behind. After Tobias sat behind it for two weeks, it wasn't quite as orderly.

Hey, you left me in charge, while you're skinny dipping in Hawaii. What did you expect?

Tobias was sitting on the porch when Abby drove up and parked her SUV. She got out with the daily mail in her hand.

"Hey, you got some mail."

"Me? If it's a bill, give it to Deacon."

"It's not a bill. In fact, it looks like it was written with colored pencil. Very creative."

Tobias held out his hand as she came up the steps. When she handed it to him, he looked at the carefully printed lettering, alternating colors with each letter.

"It's from Riley." He smiled and looked at her. "The kid wrote me a letter."

"It's so cute. Open it."

He took out his pocket knife and carefully sliced open the top of the envelope. Inside were two pieces of paper. One was a letter, and the other was a drawing of two people on a horse. At least, that's what he thought it was. It was a little hard to tell.

He looked at the letter.

Abby sat next to him. "Read it out loud."

Tobias cleared his throat. *"Dear Tobias.* Spelled T O I B A S. *How are you? I am fine. I miss you and Chance.* Spelled without the E. *What have you been doing? I have been at school, but now it is over."* He glanced at Abby, then continued. *"I hope I can see you and Chance again soon. I miss Abby and Tanner, too. And Cassidy.* Spelled with a T. *And Deacon.* Spelled completely wrong." He laughed. *"I drew you a picture of me and you on Chance. I hope you like it. Please write me back when you are not busy riding horses. Love, Riley."*

He picked up the picture and looked at it, then showed it to Abby. "I'm not much for crying, but if anything was going to make me cry, this would be it."

Abby hugged him. "It's adorable. You need to frame it. And you need to write him back."

He nodded, then got to his feet.

"Where are you going?"

"To town."

"Dinner is in an hour."

"I'll be back." He stepped off the porch and headed for his truck.

Abby called after him. "Can I come with?" He motioned for her to come. "I need to get my purse."

"You don't need your purse, Abby. Come on."

She jogged down the steps and over to his truck. As she got in, he pulled away.

"So, what are we doing in town?"

"We're going to Johnson's."

"Do you have a sudden urge to buy ranch supplies?"

"No. We're going to buy Riley a cowboy hat."

"Didn't he take Tanner's old one with him?"

"Yeah. But the kid deserves his own hat."

"Of course he does." She reached over and patted his knee.

They got to town, and Tobias parked in front of the store. It carried everything from feed to clothing. They went inside and made their way to the hat section, and Tobias looked around.

A clerk came up to them. "What can I help you with?"

"I need a hat for a kid. I don't know what size, but he's an average-sized six-year-old."

"I'd go with a child's medium. Unless he has an unusually large head, it should be fine. And if it's a bit big, he'll grow into it."

Tobias nodded. "Sounds good."

The clerk showed him a selection of hats ranging in colors.

Abby picked up a black one. "This one."

Tobias looked at it. "You think?"

"Yes. Because it's just like yours."

"You mean the one Gemma stole from me?"

"Yes. That one."

He smiled. "Okay. Black it is."

The clerk took it from Abby. "Good choice. Is it a gift? Would you like it gift wrapped?"

"I don't suppose you can ship it?"

"Yes. We can ship it for you."

"Perfect." Tobias took the envelope from his pocket and wrote the address on a slip of paper the clerk handed him. He glanced at Abby. "I just hope he got his address right."

Abby looked at it. "It looks like maybe Gemma wrote that part. It's legible."

"I think you're right." He handed the paper to the clerk, then took another and wrote a note to Riley. *Some men are born to be cowboys. Love, Tobias.*

They left the store, and Tobias looked across the street. "Can I buy my little sister a drink before we go home?"

Abby laughed. "Less than a year ago, you were about to beat up Skyler because you thought he got me drunk."

"I wasn't going to beat him up. I was just going to talk some sense into him."

"Right."

"And you weren't twenty-one. Now you are. And have been for three months. Do you want a drink, or not?"

"Sure." They crossed the street. "Ruthie's going to be mad that we're late for dinner."

Tobias shrugged. "She'll get over it."

He held the door for her and they went inside. Being five o'clock, it was almost empty. They sat at the bar and ordered two beers. He glanced at her. "I thought you didn't like beer."

"I've learned to appreciate it. I just don't like cheap beer."

"Okay." The bartender set two drafts in front of them and Tobias held his up. "To being twenty-one."

Abby tapped his glass. "Not much different from twenty."

"Except for the beer."

She drank some beer, then took out her phone and pointed it at Tobias.

"What are you doing?"

"Taking your picture."

"Are you going to forget what I look like when you head to college?"

"Don't remind me. No. This is for Gemma."

"Gemma?"

"Yeah. We've been texting."

He turned to look at her. "What? Since when?"

"Since she left."

"Hmm."

"Don't hmm, me. It's not like you're keeping in touch."

He turned back to the bar. "I'm giving her space to figure things out."

"Okay." She took a couple of pictures of him. "There, Tobias in his natural habitat."

"In a bar?"

"No. With a beer in his hand."

"I drink far more rum than I do beer."

Abby shook her head. "That's nothing to brag about."

"Not bragging. Just stating a fact." Wanting to steer the conversation away from Gemma, he decided to put her on the spot. "So, I haven't seen Skyler in a couple of weeks."

She sighed. "He's dating some woman his parents set him up with."

"A woman, huh?"

"Yes. She's older than him. And she's kind of a bitch."

Tobias laughed. "You've met her?"

"Yeah. I ran into them at the grocery store. They were buying groceries together. How domesticated is that?"

Tobias took a drink, then looked at her. "She probably picked up on the fact Skyler would rather be with you than her."

"That's not it. She's not even pretty."

"Looks aren't everything."

"Says the man who's in love with a beautiful woman."

"I'm not in love. And the fact Gemma is beautiful is an added bonus. There's a lot more to her than a pretty face and a...never mind."

Abby nudged him. "You are in love with her. And she's in love with you. And the sooner you two get over yourselves, the sooner you can be together."

Tobias finished his beer and stood up. He dropped some money on the bar, then looked at Abby. "We should get home before Ruthie has a cow."

Abby followed him to the door. "Thanks, by the way, for talking to Deacon about me going back to school."

"I talked to him. He didn't listen." He glanced at her. "I'm sorry. I know you don't want to go back." He held the door for her.

Abby went through it. "I know you tried. He did agree to a compromise. He said I need to go this year. And if I still feel this way in the spring. He'll let me drop out."

"See, I helped."

"You didn't help, Tobias. It was the tears that did it."

"You suckered him in with fake crying?"

"No. The tears were real. But he's like you. He can't stand to see a woman cry. Even if it's his sister."

Chapter Twenty-Five

"Who are you, and what did you do with my brother?"

G emma was sitting in a small fence-off area behind the clinic, where she and her colleagues could take their breaks when the weather was nice. She had the space to herself until Felicity, a fellow therapist, came out and joined her.

She held up a lunch tote. "Do you mind if I sit with you?"

Gemma smiled. "Of course not."

She sat and took a sandwich, an apple, and a can of soda from her tote. "So how's it going, Gemma?"

"Good. No complaints."

"Hmm. I think maybe that's not completely true."

Gemma had worked with Felicity for two years. She didn't see her socially, but they'd become close at work. She'd become a confidant of sorts, but Gemma had never shared any information about Tobias. In fact, she hadn't told anyone about Tobias.

"What do you mean?"

"It seems to me you're not very happy these days."

"Of course I am. I love my job. I love working with you. We get to work with young college athletes. What's not to love? I'm as happy as I can be."

"Hmm."

"Stop." Gemma looked at her. "What makes you think I'm not happy?"

Felicity set her sandwich down. "I have no doubt you love what you do. But I do doubt you're happy doing it here lately."

"Where else would I go? Am I about to get fired?"

Felicity laughed. "Of course not. This is my observation only. It seems to me you've been distracted since you came back from your trip in the spring."

Gemma nodded. "Okay. I'll admit I've been slightly distracted."

Felicity turned toward her. "By what? Or should I say by who?"

"What makes you think it's a who?"

"Because I don't think you'd let anything else interfere with your job."

Gemma took a breath. Maybe it was time to talk about it. "Okay. Let me tell you a little story."

Felicity rested her chin on her hand. "I'm listening."

"Have you ever spent time in rural Texas?"

"Nope. Not a rural girl. I've driven through it on the way to Dallas or Houston."

"Not the same." Gemma took a drink from her water bottle. "My trip in the spring was going to my friend's wedding. I was her maid of honor."

"Right. I knew that."

"She moved to Connelly a little over a year ago. It's on the Texas panhandle, practically in Oklahoma. She met and fell in love with a local rancher. She comes from a ranching family, but she grew up here in Austin. Anyway. She met a wonderful man. He's very wealthy, which is beside the point. And I had a really good time. The ranch is beautiful. The area is beautiful. I even rode a horse."

"So, you want to move to rural Texas?"

Gemma laughed. "That would just be part of it. You see, this wonderful man my friend married has an equally, but in a different way, wonderful brother."

Felicity nodded. "Gotcha. You have the hots for a rich cowboy. That explains a lot."

"Well, that's a little simplistic, but yes."

Felicity studied Gemma for a moment. "So, why are you still here?"

"I have a job. This job. I love this job. I went to school for this job. I also have a son."

"Who, I'd guess, would love to move to a ranch with a real live cowboy."

Gemma smiled. "He did love it, yes. And you're right. He'd go in a minute."

"So, again. Why are you still here?"

"Did you not hear the part about the job? There isn't a physical therapy clinic within a hundred miles of Connelly."

"Rich cowboy, right?"

"That doesn't mean I'm going to move there and expect him to take care of me."

"Okay. I understand that. But maybe you're missing an opportunity. Just because there are no clinics nearby, it doesn't mean there aren't people who need a physical therapist. You could connect with the local doctor. It seems you'd stay busy. You could even open your own clinic. You have the credentials to do that. And I'm guessing your cowboy would loan you the money to get started."

Gemma cocked her head. "Felicity. It sounds like you're trying to get rid of me."

"Not at all. I'd miss the hell out of you. But I want you to be happy. And if this hot cowboy does it for you, then...why are you still here?"

It was a very good question and Gemma was running out of ways to answer it. She'd been staying in touch with Abby and Cassidy. And Riley and Tobias were pen pals. *How adorable was that?* But she couldn't quite let herself make the commitment. She knew he was leaving her alone because he wanted to give her time to think. It wasn't because he didn't want to talk to her. But there were times when she wished he would. Of course, she hadn't contacted him either. She was afraid to. If she heard his voice, she wouldn't be able to stop herself from leaving the next day. But the new school year was coming up. She needed to make a decision.

Tobias had been spending every spare moment over the summer working on the house. With winter only a few months away now, he had to get at least the exterior finished. He was leaning a ladder against the wall when he heard voices approaching. He moved away from the house and spotted Deacon and Tanner riding up on their horses.

He gave them a wave. "I'm not complaining, but what are you doing here?"

Deacon dismounted and looked at the house. "Are you building the whole damn house by yourself?"

"On and off. I have some of the men coming by tomorrow."

Deacon tied his horse to a tree, as Tanner got down and did the same. "Can you use a couple of extra hands?"

"Grab a hammer."

"What are we doing?"

"Laying shingles."

Tanner walked to the end of the house. "What's going on here?"

"I made the kitchen a little bigger. Added a mud room and a pantry."

Tanner walked to the other end of the house. "And what's this?"

"A third bedroom."

Deacon raised an eyebrow. "So what's a bachelor need three bedrooms and a pantry for?"

Tobias looked at him for a moment. "Are we talking? Or are we laying shingles?"

They worked for the next four hours and got the roof fully shingled. When it was about an hour from sunset, they sat on the roof with beers and admired their handiwork.

Tobias smiled. "Well, that sure went a lot faster with three sets of hands. Thank you." He looked out over the meadow. "Here he comes."

They all watched as the stallion emerged from the trees and trotted a hundred yards onto the meadow. After a few minutes, he whinnied and thirty more horses came to join him. Most of them were mares, with about a third of them being foals, or yearlings.

Deacon took a sip of beer. "You're welcome, by the way."

Tobias looked at him. "For what?"

"Passing this spot on to you. I picked it out fifteen years ago."

Tanner shook his head. "You picked it out when you were nineteen?"

"Yeah. Back when I was young and hopeful."

Tobias laughed. "What are you now?"

"Older, but still hopeful." He took a drink. "Actually, I'm very happy to be staying in the big house. Cassidy loves it. Mother needs constant supervision. And in a year, both the younger Carmichaels will be away at college."

Tanner looked at Deacon, but didn't say anything. Tobias squeezed his shoulder. "The house will be kind of empty with just you and Cassidy upstairs."

"Yeah." Deacon glanced at his brothers. "Actually, there's something I need to tell you guys." He smiled, then took a drink. "Looks like you two are going to be uncles in about eight-and-a-half months."

Tanner cheered as Tobias laughed and asked, "What happened to you riding the maybe I do, maybe I don't, fatherhood fence?"

"Cassidy and I talked about it. And I realized my hesitation was based on an unrealistic fear. And then we left it in God's hands."

Tanner grinned. "And God saw fit to make it happen right away?"

"Apparently, yes."

Tobias nudged him. "Did it have anything to do with skinny dipping in Hawaii?"

Deacon laughed. "I don't think so."

"It'd be a hell of a story to tell the kid one day."

"Yeah. I think most kids don't want to know the details of how they were conceived."

"Maybe not." Tobias raised his bottle. "Well, that's great news. And one lucky kid."

"Thank you. He, or she, will be lucky to grow up in this family."

"Damn right."

They wanted to get back to the ranch before dark, so they finished their beers and climbed down off the roof, then headed across the field toward home on horseback. Tobias trotted up next to Deacon.

"You're going to want to be spending more time at home once the kid gets here."

"Yeah. I am." Deacon glanced at Tobias. "But we have several months before that."

"I know. But I'm ready to take on whatever you don't want to do. Tanner and I can go to the auctions. I can go to your damn meetings. Just let me know what you want me to do."

"I appreciate that. We'll work our way up to it. But my office is off-limits."

"I didn't mess it up that bad."

"I've been back for almost three months and I still can't find anything."

"Fine by me. But the other stuff. The stuff that takes you on the road. I know It won't be easy for you to give up the Carmichael power."

"It's not power. It's responsibility and I've been responsible for eleven years now."

"You have. And we're all grateful. But it's time for me to help you carry that load."

Deacon looked at him. "Who are you, and what did you do with my brother?"

"Seriously, man. I'm ready."

"Okay. Tell you what. We'll send you on a trial run. There's a meeting of the Texas Cattlemen's Association next weekend in El Paso. Two days of presentations, small-talk, and cocktails."

"Well, a third of that sounds good."

"Why don't you go represent the Starlight Ranch? See what you think."

"Okay. I'm there."

Tanner cleared his throat. "If Tobias is going to be traveling more, then who's going to manage the day to day stuff? The men and...you know. All that."

Deacon smiled at him. "I'm not retiring. I'll be around."

"Right. I know. But maybe I could stay home next year and help out more, too."

Deacon pointed at him. "You're trying to hornswoggle me."

"No, I just want to do my part."

"You do plenty, kid. But right now, and for the next five years, your job is to get an education."

―――――――――❦―――――――――

Tobias was sitting on his couch with a glass of rum. Other than the beer he had earlier, it was his only alcohol for the day. Gemma had sent him a physical therapy program to follow, and he'd been trying to stick to it. But it was hard to stay motivated. It'd helped a little, though, and it'd been a while since he'd gone to bed drunk.

He picked up his phone and pulled up Gemma's number. It was something he did every night. And like every other night, he put the phone back down without dialing it. He'd know when the time was right.

He set his drink aside and picked up a notepad and a pen, then began writing his weekly letter to Riley. He wanted to tell him all about the wild horses. Someday, he'd show them to him.

Deacon's news about the baby was wonderful, and he was happy for them. But it also made him a bit envious. He'd grown close to Riley over the summer. Even though it was long distance. Next to wanting to be with Gemma, being in Riley's life was second on his list of deep desires.

Guess what Deacon, Tanner and I saw today? Wild horses. You haven't seen a beautiful horse until you've seen a wild one. The stallion is pure black with a long mane and tail that blows in the wind. It's like he's moving in slow motion. But he's fierce, and he's got a family of about thirty, who he'll protect with his life. We were on the roof of my house when they came out, which gave us a perfect view...

Chapter Twenty-Six

"Am I that unforgettable?"

T he weekend in El Paso was worse than he imagined. The best part of the trip had been the drive. Saturday night, Tobias was wondering how he was going to make it through another day. Champagne Brunch at eleven, followed by a presentation by the Meat Packers Association. He'd need to be drunk to make it through that. The presentation was followed by afternoon cocktails and hors d'oeuvres. He wondered how many of these rich bastards would then head home drunk.

He picked up his phone and texted Deacon.

How have you not become an alcoholic with all the drinking going on at these things?

A few minutes later, Deacon texted back. *That's the key. If you're the only one who's sober, you're much more likely to get what you went for in the first place.*

Of course you have a plan. You always have a plan. But how do you get through a Meat Packer's presentation and remain sober?

Sit at a table with the guys from Amarillo. The drunker they get, the funnier they are. They'll keep you entertained.

Tobias sent back a thumbs up emoji. Then set his phone aside. "Okay. I'll sit with the drunk guys from Amarillo."

He tried to get some sleep, but he hated sleeping in hotels and it reminded him of the motel in Malady Springs. This was a much nicer place. But the company was definitely better in room eleven.

As he was sitting through the presentation and trying to stay awake, Tobias glanced around the room. He wasn't able to sit with the guys from Amarillo. But he could see what Deacon was talking about. The five guys at the table were having a blast. Almost to the point of rudeness.

Instead, Tobias was at a table with two women and a man, all from San Antonio. They were intently listening to the man at the podium droning on about the rising price of beef and how to stay competitive. He reached into his pocket and took out his phone, then pulled up Gemma's number. He looked at it for a moment, and suddenly everything became clear. He knew what he had to do. It was time.

When the man at the podium took a five minute break, Tobias excused himself from the table and left the conference room. He rode the elevator to his room, then went in and packed his things. After checking out of the hotel, he got into his truck. On the way there, he'd gone through New Mexico. It was a much more direct drive. But he wasn't headed home just yet. He was going to Austin. And the route he was taking would take him right through Malady Springs.

He wanted to be rested not fresh off a boring weekend when he got to Austin. So he figured what better place to stay then the Malady Springs Motel. He just might sleep well there. He arrived at the motel just after dark and checked into a room, then went across the street to the bar. The same bartender was working and seemed to recognize him. He came over to Tobias with a smile.

"Straight rum, right?"

"That's right. Am I that unforgettable?"

The bartender nodded. "It was an interesting night. How'd that all work out for you and the lady?"

"Still working on it. Seems there's a few roadblocks we're still trying to get around."

"I'll be right back with your drink."

When he returned, Tobias nodded toward the turned-off television. "No football tonight?"

"Too early in the season."

"Right." He lifted his drink. "Thanks."

Tobias was halfway through his rum when someone came into the bar and sat a few stools down from him. He glanced over, then turned in his seat.

Gemma smiled at him. "Hey Guy."

He tipped his hat. "Ms. Girl."

The bartender noticed her and poured her a rum and coke, then set it down in front of her. "Welcome back to Malady Springs."

"Thank you." She looked at the television. "No football?"

Tobias answered for the bartender. "Too early in the season."

The bartender smiled. "I'll be at the end of the bar. If you need a refill, just holler."

Tobias looked at Gemma. "Are you going to scooch down here and tell me what the hell you're doing in Malady Springs?"

"Sounds like a ploy to me."

He took a drink. "Suit yourself. I don't care much one way or the other."

Gemma picked up her drink and moved to the stool next to Tobias. "I'm on my way to see a friend."

"A friend, huh?"

"Yeah. He's a pretty good friend. Lives in a town that makes Malady Springs look like a thriving metropolis."

"What's this friend do there?"

She sighed, then looked at Tobias' jeans, western shirt, and cowboy hat. "Well, unlike you, he's a real cowboy. Owns a little ranch."

"A *little* ranch?"

She shrugged. "Maybe it's a little bigger than little." She took a drink. "Where are you headed?"

"I'm on my way to Austin. I have a friend, too."

"A friend?"

"I'd like to change that title to something more if she's willing."

"What are you planning on saying to this friend to make her something more?"

He finished the rum in his glass. "I plan on begging her to leave her life behind, pack up her kid, and come home with me."

"Hmm. That's a big ask."

"I know. That's why I'm driving all the way to Austin to ask her in person."

"And what do you think she'll say?"

He grinned. "I think she just might be willing."

"What are you offering her? If she's giving up everything, it better be really enticing."

"Well, you see. I have this house that's almost finished. And when you sit on the deck just before the sun goes down, the wild horses come out and feed on the grass that stays green all year round because of the springs."

"Wild horses, huh?"

"Yep. When last she saw this house, it only had two bedrooms. But I added another. I also made the kitchen bigger."

"And why would a bachelor, such as yourself, need three bedrooms and a bigger kitchen?"

"Well. One room would be hers and mine. One room would be for her son. And the third...well, you see, my brother and his wife are expecting their first child. And we've always been a little bit competitive. So, I figure I'd have a jumpstart with an already hatched, fully grown six-year-old. But it wouldn't hurt to take away his thunder a little and give his kid a cousin just a few months younger."

"Wow, that's taking competition to a whole new level."

Tobias shrugged. "I'd also be fine with waiting a year or so. I'm flexible."

She turned in her seat. "Are you planning on staying the night, cowboy?"

He pulled a key out of his pocket. "Room thirteen. I tried to get room eleven, but somebody had already gotten it."

Gemma took a key from her purse. "Room eleven."

Tobias laughed. "Do you want to get out of here?"

She nodded and Tobias waved at the bartender. "Can we get our check, please?"

The bartender smiled. "It's on me, folks."

Gemma took a twenty out of her purse. "Let's make sure the bartender gets a good tip."

Tobias got to his feet and tipped his hat at the bartender, then took Gemma's arm as they headed for the door. "So, eleven or thirteen?"

"Definitely, eleven."

They went out the door and crossed the street to the motel. When they got to room eleven, Tobias took the key from her and unlocked the door. They stepped in and Gemma put her arms around his neck and pulled him in for a kiss.

He grinned as he kicked the door closed. "Hey boss lady."

Abigale' story is next. Abigale

https://www.amazon.com/dp/B0C89XX714

More Books By Leigh Fenty

The Three Oaks Ranch Series

Memories Of You

The Good Son

The Wayward Son

Little Sis

The Carmichael Series

Deacon

Tobias

Abigale
Tanner
The Christmas Wedding
Faith's Journal

The Gracie Island Series
The Deputy
The Best Woman
The Chief
The Family Man
The Visitor

Love Notes
The Last Will And Testament Of Atticus Wainwright III

The Out of Focus Series
Out Of Focus
Out Of Luck

Out Of The Deep
Out Of Time

The John O'Leary Series
The Boy In The Yellow Wellies
The Man Without A Heart

Touch
A Change Of Plans

About the Author

L eigh spends her days with cute, sexy guys. Unfortunately, they're on paper. But still, not a bad way to spend your day. She also writes about strong, independent women, who can hold their own against these irresistible guys. She's not a pure romance writer, because she breaks the rules a bit. But that's the fun part. Leigh's stories have adventure, family relationships, and the struggles life throws at you sometimes. But boy always meets girl. They tussle a bit while they figure out what they really want. Then find their happily ever after. Even if it's not what they thought it was going to be.

Printed in Great Britain
by Amazon